TLR
TAHOMA
LITERARY
REVIEW

tahomaliteraryreview.com

TAHOMA LITERARY REVIEW
Number 14
Spring 2019

ISBN-13: 978-1-942797-13-5

Copyright @ 2019 Tahoma Literary Review, LLC
Seattle ● California
tahomaliteraryreview.com

Tahoma Literary Review

Table of Contents

You can hear many of the authors in this issue read their stories, poems, and essays at https://soundcloud.com/tahomaliterary/tracks.

About This Issue

As this issue goes to production, the buzz word is "shutdown." Storms have blanketed much of the country with snow—grounding flights, delaying trains, knocking out power. It's enough to make you want to crawl into a hole and hibernate, groundhog-style.

But the twenty-five writers who contributed the poems, stories, and essays featured in this issue have opted not to hibernate, not to shut down. Instead, they're listening up and asking us to do the same. These are important voices within these pages, exploring themes of loneliness, expressing various emotions—from hubris and anger to regret and joy. Make no mistake, there's a lot of joy in these pages. And speaking of critters that hibernate, they're here, too: snakes, skunks, marmots, bees. Yet these poems, stories, and essays remain essentially human.

Which brings us to our cover—the first since we four co-owners and editors have taken the TLR reins that does not spotlight a quadrupedal or winged creature. Instead, this issue features a self-portrait of the artist, Sonia Brittain, who imbues her drawings and paintings with a love for stories and the human relationships that tie into them.

The issue begins and ends with poetry. Katherine Lo's "God's Ears" sets the stage, seeking meaning in existence, while Rachel Ronquillo Gray bows before the falling curtain after questioning expectation and reality in "Girl Gone Rogue." Woven throughout the issue, our poetry selections tell stories of exploration. Farnaz Fatemi's "Untranslated," Daniel Lusk's "Self-Portrait with Cat," and Sara Henning's "Self- Portrait as an Apostle of Longing" explore identity from different perspectives.

Roy Bentley serves as witness for "The Girl Who Survived by Pretending to Be a Corpse," while Faylita Hicks looks at survival in "Black Escapism." Daniel Lassell's "Finishing the Harvest" explores how we store and release memories, and Steven Duong's "Between Your Body and the

Boardroom" imagines how we might hold something shapeless.

In nonfiction the themes range from reflections on mental illness, as in Tyler Dunning's "The Practice of Parting Before the Farewell Even Exists," to dealing with racism, as in Charlie Brown's "I think you're wrong but." For further notes on the human experience, look to Dionne Custer Edwards' parsing of emotions in "Court of Common Pleas," Bill Capossere's interlude with spiders in "The Web," Meredith Doench's grappling with her father's memory loss, and Mary Birnbaum's encounters with aliens, gophers, and the neighbor in "Like Home."

In fiction, the issue's selections contain a healthy dose of magical realism but also reality and grit. A man in the professional cuddling business narrates his day in Jenna-Marie Warnecke's "Cuddlebug," while a young woman navigates her day using emotion coupons in AnnElise Hatjakes's "Learning to Ration." The protagonist of Eleanor Stern's "The Bargain" finds herself negotiating a world riddled with holes, and two men relive memories as they dine in "A Restaurant in Guadalajara," by José Enrique Medina. While Ta'riq Fisher's narrator in "Birds, Bees" must reckon with very real cautionary tales, fables and stories provide escape and solutions for the characters in Margot Douaihy's "Boom," Matthew Fitch's "The Tropic," Hannah van Didden's "Jezabel's Reformation," Bruce Ducker's "The Fabulist of Midtown," and Jessica Barksdale's "Storytime."

We hope you'll be as moved and changed as we were upon reading these fabulous stories, poems, and essays. Be sure to read the Contributors' Comments, where our writers describe the stories behind their featured works. Then please find us on Twitter, Amazon, or Facebook, and let us know your thoughts and reactions to this issue.

TLR

TAHOMA
LITERARY
REVIEW

God's Ears

KATHERINE LO

If an oak falls in the woods,
it always makes a sound,
at least in God's ears, a thousand
trillion listening everywhere.
Ears suspended by the slow drip
of years in the jagged stalactite
caves. Ears in the pluming puffs
of dust swirled by a late afternoon
gust. Ears in the delicate, searching
tips of the black beetle's antennae.
In the sparrows that dart and hop
on busy streets, between concrete
buildings, in oil-slicked lots.
The angels, too, can hear, though
no one thinks they're real anymore.
Or God. Even so, the guitar strings
inside keep strumming *please please.*
So many pleas. The ears listen,
hearing the fall of every last oak
in every hollow heart.

A Restaurant in Guadalajara

José Enrique Medina

Wanna eat here? I asked my brother. *There's a line, it must be good.* An hour later, a waiter served me an oval plate with golden potato medallions and enchiladas glazed in a red salsa that opened my sinuses in starts and spurts, until I was back in Mama's kitchen, licking my lips at her dishes. But—youth never tasted so good. *This is the best meal,* Turo said. Like men who can't stop talking about the earthquake that, minutes before, shifted their house, we focused the conversation on the enchiladas, on the delicate skin of the tortillas, on the spices in the secret sauce that, like long fingers, touched forgotten keys, taking music out of pianos that we had thought were abandoned or destroyed. We remembered the past. Polished in red salsa, it was more beautiful the second time.

THE FABULIST OF MIDTOWN

BRUCE DUCKER

1.

The night lobby put him in mind of an old radio show: the clip-clop of his leather-soled cordovans could have been a sound man. A woman was sitting at the security desk with Ernie. In the airiness of marble and glass, her lipstick shone crimson.

"Done for the night," he said, a commonplace he often called to Ernie on the way out. Tonight he added, "Enough for one day."

"Time to go home, Mr. Bergson," Ernie's line. He'd answer, See you tomorrow.

But not tonight. Tonight he walked over.

"Hi." He pretended to notice her. "You're new."

"Only here," she smiled, a slight overbite, Riding Hood's wolf. "Mostly I'm the old me." A blue-gray uniform, her face a painting, he couldn't think of the artist, olive skin, gray eyes that stayed lit. On the nape of her neck, from the collar, snaked a tattoo rosebud about to bloom.

Had he ever talked to a tattooed woman? He couldn't pull his sight from the bud—he thought to get his mouth around it and bite it off.

Words were needed. "Well, you'll see a lot of me. Right Ernie? I tend to work late."

Ernie took it up. "These lawyers all do. Their clients must be in jail."

He was stuck on the flower. She noticed. He let go a little chuckle, intended to charm. It came out goofy.

"I'm not that kind of lawyer," he said, hoping she would hit the ball back: Well, what kind are you, and they'd be off and running.

She declined the gambit. "Well," she allowed, "you know what they say."

He didn't know what they say. He rarely dated, often saw women he'd like to meet but didn't quite go about it.

"All work and no play?"

She sniffed. Sorry he'd missed the jackpot? "Use it or lose it."

Tax law taught the importance of planning, but he'd neglected to get her name.

After that he left only during the night shift. She came on at eight. Ernie was always with her, she reading. At their second meeting he asked.

Strindberg, Odets, Boleslavski.

Again he was thrown. These names—if he'd read them in college, he'd forgotten. So he Googled. The next night, she was reading Beckett.

"You're studying to be an actress?"

"I *am* an actress."

She scared him—neither the lines nor the scene was familiar, only the sensation. In the movie of his life, he felt like a body double.

That's how it went for several weeks. Once he commented on *End Game*. "It seems so bleak …" The words came out lame—why hadn't he tried them before a   mirror?—and she moved her brow, as if she was dealing with a child first noticing clouds. But no other response.

He worked late even when not busy. He slept in, went to the office about noon, and, until he could see her, browsed websites. Sure-Fire Opening Lines, the World's Best Love Poems.

Picking out his clothes for the day was the best part of the job. One morning he put on a favored suit, a medium gray with a pencil stripe of cream, and a festive tie.

"Ernie. A bunch of kids are hanging out on the Lex Avenue side. Just hanging around."

"I'll take a look," Ernie reached for his cap. Groaned, tamped down his white moustache with a lower lip.

She spoke up. "You stay, Ernie. I'll go."

"I'll walk with you," Adam invented. His plan was that Ernie would leave them alone. "I exit that way."

They started across the granite floor.

Ernie called: "Let me know if you need help, sweetheart." She smiled again.

The yearning in Adam's chest made his fingers tremble. He put his hands in his pockets. You can't go on inventing kids who are hanging out.

"I'm Adam."

"Like, with Eve?"

"No. Not like that. I'm without Eve. We had a thing for a while."

"What happened?"

"Scared of snakes."

At last the smile he wanted.

"Bummer," she said after another stage silence, "for Cain and Abel."

"You like your job?"

"It's OK."

"Boring?"

"Except for kids in the Lex Avenue lobby."

"Happens a lot?"

"First time." They were almost there, where his extemporization ended.

Points of contact, that's what he needed. "My job can be boring too. God, can it ever." There were of course no kids. If this were theater he thought to say, there would be. "Know what I do? When it's boring?"

"No," she answered. Her voice played over a chord of suspicion, the tone city women use against—what?—flattery? a sex nut? a friend?

"I daydream."

Surprised, her head bobbed in approval. "My grampa used to say?" she asked him, "about dreaming?"

"No, what?"

"You can dream about dumplings. But come dinner, they're still a dream, not dumplings."

"I don't dream about food," he said. "I dream stories. I sit in an office that costs my firm a fortune in rent, dreaming up stories." If only he could hypnotize her.

"Like what?"

He crooked his finger, Come. They walked to the plate glass facing the street. He was one sentence further than the script.

"See that store?" The shop across Lexington was closed. Over its façade the sign was unlit: Avenue Deli.

"Every day at noon a young woman comes to that deli and sits at the counter. She has a kind face but plain. She goes because she is mad for the grill guy. He wears black tee shirts, his skin is smooth, the color of coffee with real cream. When he's cooking he wears an apron against the grease. When he takes it off to work the counter he reminds her of a bullfighter. She watches to see him do it. Her name is Lucille and his name, although she does not yet know it, is Carlos.

"One day, after she orders fried-egg-sandwich-glass-of-milk, she puts up her hand, wait. He waits, holds a ball-point pen upright, over his order pad.

"'You're always here,' she tells him. 'Don't you get time off?'

"'Yes, I get.'

"'When?'

"'Whenever I want.' A customer has never asked about him. "'I never want.'

"'Why not?'

"Carlos the beautiful counterman shrugs. 'No reason. Nowhere to go.'

"''Ask tomorrow. We'll do something.'

"'Nice,' Carlos says and tilts his head. In a drought this idea is rain. 'Meet you here at one.'"

An electronic crackle made Adam jump. The guard unclipped her hand-held from her belt. Ernie was making sure she was all right.

"Yeah," she said to the sound. "No kids. But an elevator stuck on twenty-three. I'll check it out." She clicked off the machine and turned to Adam.

"So what happens?" she asked. "Lucille and Carlos."

"It's a long story."

She studied him, lapidary eyes disappearing behind narrowing lids. He remembered once touring some Norman castle. Its battlements were shuttered so you could shoot out, but only a perfectly aimed arrow would fit in.

"I'm going to twenty-three," she said and jerked her head, Follow me. He trailed along.

She had him wait while she went into the car, turned a key in the control panel.

"What's that all about?"

"Shuts down the camera." She pointed to the corner. A light winked red.

"Ernie shouldn't see you. Wouldn't understand."

"Won't he notice the camera's off?"

"Happens." She hit the button. The doors closed and the car began to move. "So?"

When Lucille got to the deli, ten minutes early, Carlos was at the grill. It glistened: strips of bacon, two burgers sizzled. Carlos scraped together a mess of eggs and turned them. The heat was on high, everyone was in a rush, and the place popped with static.

"Be right witcha," he said without turning around. The counter stools were filled. Some women left a booth, and Lucille sat on the edge of its bench. Carlos slid the burgers to buns, shoveled fries to one plate and onion rings to a second. He scooped the bacon to a third plate, heaped on the eggs. From a stash towards the back of the grill he added a spatula of home fries.

The apron was off in a single move.

"Gus," he called, "I'm off." Lucille hadn't noticed Gus before. She hadn't noticed much outside of Carlos. The owner sat on a stool behind the cash register, a heavy, mournful man in a sweatshirt that read Athletic Department. From his perch he could see the To-Go line, empty seats, what cash got left.

Carlos came over, put two glasses of water on the table, and slid into the booth across from her. Handed her a menu.

"So," he said. "We'll score some chow and do something."

"Great," Lucille replied.

A waitress lifted the water glasses to swipe a dish towel across the table.

"You take the grilled cheese or the fried egg or the tuna fish," he told Lucille. "And a milk."

"Yes," she said, although she wanted a moment to think. Nothing that dripped. No dressing on salad, no tuna smell. Without his remark, she might have splurged. Turkey and Swiss with Russian dressing, the avocado club.

"I'll have a grilled cheese."

"No fries, Gloria. She takes slaw instead." That he knew thrilled her. "Me," he said, "I'm a meat and potatoes man. Steak sandwich with onions, large Coke. She's a milk."

"I'm not a milk," Lucille spoke up. "I'm a woman. And I'd like coffee."

"Hey, good," Carlos told her when the waitress left. "You're a woman, not a milk." He laughed and she could see teeth the size of dice at the back of his mouth.

On twenty-three, the stuck elevator, someone had left a law book so the doors wouldn't close.

"They do that," she told Adam. "Lawyers. They don't want to wait for an elevator. They want it to wait for them."

She placed the book in the hall. The doors of the car closed.

"God," Adam said sympathetically. "What assholes. That's not my firm, you know."

"I know. You're on thirty-six."

They began a tour of the empty floor.

Carlos guided her out of the deli as if she didn't know the way. Lucille noticed he'd left a five-dollar bill for the waitress. "We get the discount," he told her, "but you can't take that out of Gloria's hide."

They walked in the autumn sun. Up Lexington and west. They stood outside the children's zoo at a low fence and watched *au pairs* watching their kids. A crowd surrounded the seal pool, cheering. "Feeding time," she said.

"I never been here before," Carlos said. "This is pretty cool. Does it cost?"

"Yes, but not much. I'll pay."

"No way. You're not paying. We'll come back. I'll hit a number, we'll come back."

Lucille was thrilled. It wasn't quite a date, lunch at his job and a walk through the park. If he paid, that would be a date.

On the way back they came down Fifth for the store windows. Some were dressed for Christmas but most still had their fall displays.

"I heard about these but I never seen them before."

"How long have you lived in New York?"

"All my life. Twenty-eight years. Not so much New York as the Bronx."

"That's New York," she corrected him.

"Ditmas Avenue, that's not New York."

"So how is it you've never seen Fifth Avenue or the Zoo?"

"I work on Lex, take the train both ways. Gets me right there." Carlos shared an apartment with two brothers and their families. In the living room, his bed turned into a sofa for daytime.

"I have my own place," Lucille said. It was a forward thing to say, but she didn't care. He was kind and funny. That was all she wanted. In high school when they discussed the ideal boyfriend, they'd say rich, handsome, responsible. Words from magazines.

"So?" She asked back at the elevator. "Is that all?"

"No. The best is ahead."

She pressed the L button and waited.

Lucille walked him back to work, linking her arm in his. At the corner, she stopped. She could see the orange sign, *Deli*. "I enjoyed this," Carlos said and stuck out his hand. She took it; it seemed warmed from the grill. They stood in the birdsong of horns and whooshing cars.

"I never asked you. What are you interested in? I mean, cooking, I know. But what else?"

"I play the numbers. Cost you a quarter. You hit, you win a grand. Hit big it's more."

"What would you do with the money?"

His eyes were impatient. He looked up at the buildings. "Get out," he said. "Get out of here."

Lucille was disappointed. She admired his resolve, but she was hoping for something romantic.

"So." The light changed again, people around them moved south. "So. What next?" Drippings of the last daylight ran to the bottom of the street. She wished she'd seen him more. They had walked side by side so she hadn't been able to watch his face.

"We'll do this again," Carlos said easily for both of them. "This was great."

"Do I get to hear more?" They left the elevator and walked to the Lexington exit. The revolving doors were latched. They moved to the heavy glass fire doors on the end. Adam pushed the bar and moved the door into the November wind.

"I don't know your name," he said.

"But I know yours. That's a start." Her eyes flashed in fun and he smiled.

"May I touch that wonderful tattoo?" He raised his hand towards her face, gentle as a sparrow. She caught it mid-flight.

"Perhaps later." Now her turn to smile

"We'll do this again," he said. "This was great."

2.

For all Adam's education, the impression he gave—a callow tourist with full purse and no purpose—was not without truth. The next evening that she was on, Adam stayed late.

At about eleven he wandered down to the lobby. He said hi. Ernie was there too. He couldn't tell whether they were welcoming.

"Do you get time off for a walk?" he asked her.

She shook her head slowly. "Eight hours straight through."

"Not even a break?"

"I get breaks. But you're not allowed in the ladies room."

Ernie kept reading the Post. "Do a circuit, take him," he said for Adam to hear. "Take him on the twelve."

"Not allowed," she said, all the time her eyes on Adam.

"Ah, what the hell," said Ernie. "You find a burglar, he'll take the bullet."

The idea made her smile. She was enjoying this. Had they rehearsed it?

"You want, come along. I do a circuit at twelve. Another at three."

"Sure," Adam said. "I'll do the twelve. What is it?"

"Midnight. I walk a few floors. Security, separate copulating accountants, that sort of thing. Stop the cleaning crews from stealing the trash."

He was back early, and waited while she finished a chapter in her book.

"Come, then," she said and rose.

"Where you going, Selena?" Ernie was working the crossword.

She read from a printout. "Seventeen, twenty-four, thirty-one. And…," she said with a sly glance at Adam, "thirty-six."

"That's my floor," Adam said.

They were silent on the way to the elevators.

"Ah," he said when the doors closed. "Selena. That's pretty. Does it mean something?"

"Depends who you ask."

"Not that. I meant…"

She let him off. "Moon. It's Greek for moon."

"That's perfect. Beautiful, remote…"

"Landed on more than once," she replied. "Barren and airless. Also, every visitor leaves their crap behind."

He was not dissuaded. "Circling overhead, just out of reach."

"And every so often it disappears."

"But it comes back."

She thought on this, pursing her lips, and answered after the bell for the floor. "So far." And again held the door for him. Something was growing in him, and Selena was its seed. The voice he used through life was small and precise, but he could feel it growing in timbre.

Only fire stair signs lit the corridor. At first he saw nothing. It was an eerie, movie-effects sensation—long shafts of air illuminated by one green word: Exit. A mixture of intimacy and menace. Selena moved routinely to the switching panel and turned a key. The overheads came on. He found himself blinking, blinded anew.

"So," she said to cue him, "Carlos and Lucille."

Adam had rehearsed the story, the very words and rhythms.

Lucille spent a miserable few days. All she could think of was Carlos, the grace of his body. When he moved his head, the long muscles of his neck showed like a sprinter's. That week she continued to take her lunch at the counter, but Carlos was busy on the grill and could only wave, which he did. Finally, on a Friday, she gathered her nerve and bent her finger to call him. He carried a metal spatula.

"What do you think?" she asked. "Next week?"

"Tuesday." His voice was neither encouraging nor familiar, but the word did its work. "Tuesday, same drill."

"Meet you here?"

He nodded. She left elated but wondering whether they would be seeing each other if she hadn't spoken up.

On Tuesday they ate lunch at the deli and she ordered the grilled cheese and coleslaw, while he got the avocado club. "That looks great," she told him, staring at a triangle, bacon and mayo slipping from its crust, the toast held together with a red-crested toothpick. But he didn't offer. Simply downed it and drank his mug of coffee, ordered a slab of blueberry pie.

Afterwards they walked. The weather was cooler, with a wind. They went down Madison and across Forty-second to a free exhibit at the public library. In glass cases, magazines from the Sixties and Seventies lay open to display cartoons. They argued over which were funny and why. Many referred to people and events that meant nothing to them. A guard explained Watergate.

Lucille felt secure and special. They were a tribe of two, and the locals had to teach them the island culture. They walked down the steps together.

"See those lions," she pointed to the sculptures on either side. "They're named Patience and Fortitude."

"No shit?" She nodded. She had looked them up.

"What are they doing?"

"They're protecting the library." Carlos chewed at his lower lip in thought.

"Somebody's going to steal books?" he asked and she laughed. A block later he turned to her. "Fortitude. What does that mean?"

Lucille was unprepared. "It's sort of, the ability to wait."

"No, that's patience."

"Well, fortitude." She had never said the word before, liked its sound. "More like, you can stick it through. Hard times? Troubles? No matter what?"

Carlos sucked on his lip and produced a rubbery squeak.

"Isn't that something?" he asked.

"What?"

"Well, that could be me. Patience and fortitude. I never heard of it, and it's me. Makes you wonder what other words there are."

Again they ended catty-corner from the deli. He had to work the last hours; mostly To-Go, he told her, for delivery to surrounding offices. She turned towards the building where she worked; people poured out of it, drab, sullen; time and tedium had leeched the color from their faces.

"Why do these people work so hard?" Selena asked him on a circuit.

"They like it," he said.

"The money?"

"The money, and it takes up time. No time left for…"

"For life," she said.

"You ever noticed," he asked on another floor, "how city people move in straight lines? Up, down, one way streets. Like the rook on a chess board." She shrugged and told him, Go back to the story.

It went on for several weeks. What Carlos did on the week-ends and why he never asked her out, she didn't know. She knew only about herself; her heart was on fire. Sometimes she could feel its heat rise in her lungs. On Saturdays, across the river in Brooklyn, she shopped, went to the bank, ironed blouses to the opera broadcast. Sundays she read a paperback, watched movies on a Goodwill TV, did her checkbook. Considered how she was preparing for a future that, except for ironing and laundry and radio broadcasts of *La Boheme*, was obscured.

Still. Walking with Carlos, she found pleasure in the expressions of other people, their reaction to his face and carriage. She saw them recognize how she loved him, and their approval. Often when they walked together, an older woman would catch her eye, nod privately, and smile.

Maybe she'd cook him dinner. They might walk about Prospect Park, visit the museum. But she couldn't work up the nerve.

"That's what I don't like about the story," Selena said.

"What is?"

"She's so shy. She hasn't the *cojones* to be a hero."

"I never said she was a hero. She is who she is."

That didn't satisfy Selena. She wanted more action, but Adam said it again, We are who we are.

3.

Adam joined her regularly on her rounds. He'd resolved that the romance go somewhere. He expected it, Lucille expected it, and Selena was growing impatient. At the same time he was careful of Selena's feelings, building momentum.

They arrived at his firm's office, two floors. The halls seemed darker than the others. Adam caught his breath at the strangeness, familiar shapes in black. She hesitated before turning the switch. Lights came on, ceiling panels every twenty feet covered by an identical plastic lens. All the lines were regular.

The upper floor housed the corporate people, who worked late, and the litigators, who worked around the clock. On his floor were lawyers doing trusts and tax planning, property conveyances—people inclined to take life as they found it.

As the lobby brought to mind old radio dramas, he imagined these halls as a space ship. The doomed one in the Kubrick movie. Silence framed by the hum of airless speed, vast, unpeopled spaces. He liked the fantasy—it suggested that he, despite forty stories of steel and concrete and glass footed into a stone island, he was making progress.

She interrupted.

"So which is your office?"

They turned a corner and he put out his hand, Ta-*da*, to indicate a darkened room. She flashed a beam inside, reached around the doorjamb and flicked the switch. Papers stacked on his desk, books left open, overstuffed accordion files the burnt red of clay.

On the walls hung framed diplomas; two, he noticed self-conscious-ly, in   Latin. "Hmm," she looked around, "can't fool around on that desk."

Adam laughed. Before he could respond, she had turned out the lights and walked on. He looked into the space and understood he had this office not for love of the law but for timidity.

On thirty-one the cleaning crew was at work. Radios played mariachi at top volume. Vacuums thrummed and dragged black cords behind them like tails.

"I'll give you a story," she said on the ride down. "My grampa's. Once upon a time, an eagle's egg got in a hen's nest. Don't ask how. The eaglet grew up with chicks. He thought he was a chicken. He clucked and cackled, and scratched the ground for feed.

"One day, a shadow passed over. He looked up and saw a giant bird in the sky. Wide wings, a bird who could swoop. Awed, the eagle-chicken asked 'What is that?'

"The rooster told him, 'That's the eagle, king of birds. Eagles live in the sky; but we chickens live only on the earth.' And so the eagle that believed he was a chicken lived like a chicken, and one day he died like one."

Adam walked her back.

"What's the play you're reading?"

"It's about three women. All the same, different ages. One near the end, a second in mid-life, and the third young, like me.

"They've called me back for a second audition."

"I'll come see you."

"I don't have the job. Besides," she said, "it's not New York, it's out-of-town. I'm reading for C., the youngest. She's twenty-six, brash, ballsy. She's determined not to become like the old woman, senile and bitter."

At the desk Ernie sat turning pages of newspaper.

"Does she succeed?"

"Doesn't tell yet."

"Will you let me know?"

Selena picked up the play script. "Sure," she said.

4.

These were not easy times for Adam. Lucille and Carlos must make some progress. Too, he had lost interest in his work. Until Selena appeared, work had moored him to the long littleness that passes the hours. Now he lived for three people, two of them fictitious.

The next day he arrived at the office exhausted, and sat looking out the window at chaotic clouds that threatened to drown uptown. He attempted no work until after lunch. Buildings lined the view and calibrated the dark skies. At noon, he ate a sandwich at his desk and turned to a corporate reorganization. But an hour into the effort he lifted all the papers from his desk, scattered them on the floor, and lay down on the bare wood surface.

Not to sleep, but to dream. Yet he must have closed his eyes, for the next thing he knew he was staring at the partner who had given him the corporate reorg problem.

"Adam, are you all right?"

He stirred. The dream popped and vanished, impossible to piece back together.

Selena let him know to continue the story. And so he did, arriving at eleven forty-five that night, for the midnight circuit. She rose as he neared the desk and jangled her ring of keys.

"Carlos and Lucille," she spoke without looking back. "Are they ever going to get it on?"

"I don't know. The story isn't over. How did the audition go?"

"Bad, I didn't land the part. They already cast it. But good, I might get understudy."

"That'd be great. When will it be? I'll come see you."

She turned, holding a door that needed no holding, and regarded him so that he felt conspicuous. He liked the feeling. All he knew about the world was one particular legislative code, its coverts and byways. It was make-believe, unreal except that everyone paid heed to it. But it was without flesh, dimension.

"You can't, silly. I told you. It's not here. You'd have to quit your job." The idea made his insides sink, like a fast elevator. "Anyway," she went on, "back to the story."

Lucille and Carlos are now seeing a lot of each other. She invites him to Brooklyn, a bright Saturday in December, sharp and cold, and they walk on the promenade by the Bridge. Other couples, some pushing strollers. A man pulls an oxygen tank behind him. Lovers hold hands, and Lucille envies them, the warmth of their faces.

They stop at a pushcart and buy Polish sausages on buns. The works: fried cabbage, tomatoes and onions. They eat on a bench and drink coffee out of white cardboard cups. It is the best lunch Lucille has ever had. Across the river, lower Manhattan stands unused and silent, in storage until Monday.

Carlos dances about, breathing in the smell of the sea and pointing out the great bridge he walked across to get here.

"Why didn't you take the train?"

"That train goes under the river. I seen it on the map. Who thought of that?"

She guesses. "Did you mind crossing the bridge?"

He twists at the iron armrest of the bench as if to wrench it loose. "I don't like heights. 'Specially heights over water."

"You can cure that, you know. With hypnosis. Perhaps," by now she does not worry so much about what she says, "perhaps I should hypnotize you."

He smiles. Wipes his hands a last time, crumples the scalloped paper plates, sticks them into an emptied cup. Turns and tosses the mass of cardboard and fried cabbage into a wire trash basket. Then he swings his feet onto the bench, laces his fingers on his chest, and lowers his head to her lap.

She touches a napkin to her tongue and from the corners of his lips dabs traces of tomato sauce. As if he's a child, whispers, "Close your eyes." She speaks softly, tells him her lap is a raft and he cannot fall out.

"Now tell me about your voyage to Brooklyn."

"I took the train. Underground." On his brow she sees the anxiety of rocking cars and black tunnels, lights speeding by.

"Then what?"

"I got off at Nassau. Early, so's I'd have time to walk across the bridge."

"Why? Why didn't you stay on the train?"

"The train goes under the river. I didn't want to be around for that."

"Tell me about walking over the bridge."

"I was scared. I thought it would be okay but it wasn't. When you're in a building you don't know how high you are until there's no building. On the bridge some places the sidewalk is like a fence."

"A grate."

"A grate. You look down at water between your feet."

"Why did you come?"

"There's this beautiful woman on the other side waiting for me."
Here he opens his eyes, the color of seal, the color of quicksilver. Lucille lifts
her knees to raise his head to her. When she bends to kiss him her coat gets
in the way, but she pushes down the folds and kisses him. He tastes of tomato
sauce and sweet onion.

They walk to her apartment while the light of the day dwindles.
Before she met him today, she put on clean sheets. After they make love, they
lie on the bed while the darkness settles around the shapes of their bodies.
They tell about themselves. She owns three movies on DVD and says, Pick
one we'll watch—they are her favorites. He says no, I want to watch you, so
you tell them. She describes *Now Voyager*. Bette Davis is a wallflower who
meets a man on a cruise to Rio. She tells him of *Random Harvest* too, and of
Brief Encounter.

All the time rubbing his smooth brow, she tells him a story. She says
it is the saddest story she's ever heard. It's about an eagle who goes through
life believing he's a chicken.

At this Selena whipped about in the lighted corridor to confront him.

"She told him Grampa's story?" Her voice rose with excitement and
intrigue.

Lucille asks about the future, and Carlos says he will travel. Did she
know that there are magical places? He's seen it on TV, a plateau in New
Mexico, the corner of Kauai where the road ends, and the Crestone Needle
in Colorado. Mysterious drawings in sandstone.

"Is that where you'd go?" she asks him.

"No, I want to be on the edge of the sea."

"On Vancouver Island," she says, reading his thoughts, "you can
watch storms push against the shore. Shining hills of water the size of whales."

Before dawn, he gets up, dresses, kisses the top of her head, leaves.

Selena and Adam finished their rounds and walked to the darkened lobby by
Lexington.

"How did you like it?" he asked.

"I did. All except that part about her knowing his thoughts."

"You can know someone's thoughts," Adam said. "If you think about
them all the time, you can dream their dreams. That's the point."

"So what happens next?" Across the avenue, someone had neglected
to turn off the orange *Deli* sign. "Ernie," into the hand-held. "Ernie. Unlock-
ing to check outside."

Ernie came back in a metallic squeak. "Copy that."

They went out. Ice-black air from the Maritimes blew down the streets. Adam put his arm around her as they crossed. They stood at the deli and looked inside.

"So what happens next?"

That Monday Lucille cannot wait to see him. She squeezes by the To-Go line. At the grill they are preparing lunches for conference tables.

Carlos is not there. When Gus breaks from register she catches his eye.

"Carlos," she says.

"Called in. Quit."

Gus handles a deck of sandwiches, plastic bowls. He packs a brown paper bag.

"Quit?"

"He hit a number. So he quit."

"Did he say why?"

"Leaving town."

"Moving where?"

Gus chalks prices on the bag, carries over, circles the sum.

"Moving. Vancouver." He punches the cash register.

"Vancouver."

"It's in Canada."

"That's it? That's the whole story?"

They turned to re-cross the street. There were no cars.

"No, not at all. The story goes on."

"I hope the hell."

"Oh, it does." Overhead, ridges of concrete trapped a lopsided moon. He pointed. "Look. A vagabond moon."

"Why vagabond?"

"Watch it. Another minute it'll disappear behind those buildings."

"Another minute, my ass freezes off." She leaned into him and he tightened his arm around her. Sure enough, downtown near Murray Hill, the moon drifted across the cramped corridor, measurable against the edges of skyline.

"It sprung a leak, it's sinking."

"It is," Adam said into her ear. "In Jersey they keep an emergency truck. They patch it and fill it with air."

Craning her neck made her dizzy.

"Not even round. It's been handled once too often."

People speak of the heart as if all nerve endings gather there. Adam's ache wandered through his body. It hid in the back of his throat, in a soundless cry that lodged there, or it filled his lungs, or shot through his gut, indigestible.

He thought to kiss her, but she detached and moved quickly. Inside, she pulled out her hand-held to let Ernie know they were back.

5.

At work, his memo on the reorganization had returned to his desk, covered with blue-inked comments. The words meant nothing to him. He opened a blank Word document to finish the story of Lucille and Carlos. The ending would be a happy one.

After eight, he printed his pages and wandered down to see Selena. She wasn't there.

Ernie grimaced as he approached.

"She on tonight?"

"She's gone, Mr. Bergson. Didn't she tell you?"

That was all Ernie knew. Not a last name, not an address, not whether she got the part.

Adam went to his office. Emailed requests had mounted; everyone had a tax question. Some he answered, others he told to look up the law. He was waiting, so he printed a few and went to the firm's library.

He worked until sunrise. Light-headed, he walked into the lobby as its brightness gave way to a flimsy morning. The day guard sat at the desk, and Adam engaged him. Yes, he knew Selena. But nothing more.

Adam was at the deli as it opened. He ate his way through scrambled eggs, double home fries, toasted bagel, refills of coffee.

"Anything else?" the waitress asked, already writing his check.

"A guy who used to work here? Carlos? Dark, good-looking?"

"Not since I been here."

"And you've been here…?"

"Eleven years. Can you believe it? Know how many 'hold-the-potatoes' that is?"

"How 'bout the owner? Greek man, fifty-ish. Black moustache, named Gus?"

"You got the wrong place," she said and put the check by Adam's mug. "Owner's Lebanese. Head shaved. Maybe your age."

He tried the guard service. He ran a classified in *Variety*: "Selena: Call me. Adam." No answers. He tried the Actors Guild for a woman named Selena. They wouldn't talk to him.

On a whim, he searched all three Vancouver papers online. In one, a theatre announced its next production—Edward Albee's *Three Tall Women*—tickets available, advanced sale.

Between Your Body and the Boardroom

Steven Duong

I consider letting you run late, for a brief
minute your brain running its wash cycle
as the sun pulls itself through the curtains and sets
whole continents adrift on the puddle
between your shoulder blades. If we lie here
long enough, I will witness the rise and fall
of oceans, planes of hard light crashing into
one another and settling on your back—
in time, turtles and fish will colonize
our husks, seeding those bones with color and
motion, burying whole generations
in the seafloor, and you will miss your meeting.
One freckle below your neck bobs like a lifeboat,
moored only to the ebb and flow of your breath.

I THINK YOU'RE WRONG BUT

Charlie Brown

If you asked my mother, she'd tell you I had a problem with authority figures when I was young. But I promise this wasn't that. I stood, trying my best to hide the fact that my fist was clenched, while my boss was giving me the pleasure of his opinion on racism and its existence. I tried my best to ignore those looks of "you really gonna take this from this man" that everyone who passed seemed to be giving me, and I listened. I kept thinking to myself, *Maybe this is my chance to educate him on how things really are. He just hasn't gotten the information, hasn't heard stories from someone who was on the inside of this.* So I told him about my personal experiences, and the way I've felt when I've been forced to feel like nothing more than my skin. And he sat there, with this smug smirk below his gray mustache. And this look on his face like "I'ma learn you today, boy." And proceeded to tell me about how hard his upbringing was. And that struggle has never had anything to do with color. And the people in the stories that I told him, they weren't at all racist, simply ignorant. And maybe they had bad hearts. But it's not about skin. It's never about skin. That's all in the past now. How long ago was slavery?

I was in the fourth grade when I first came to know love. Looking back, I'm not sure what it was about her. In grade school I'd had plenty of (what we all thought were) girlfriends (at the time). Those girls with whom I spent no time at all, but I thought were cute. We'd stare across a field or playground, making eyes at each other, while she was with her friends and I was with mine. And those friends would tease and berate us as we crossed that field, that seemed so much longer now, just to give each other a quick kiss before running back to our friends, without even a glance back. But this was different.

She was new, planting herself in the midst of our chaotic class, midyear. Our teacher sat her next to me. Why me? I'm not sure. (Probably because it was the only desk open.) But in the fourth grade, I called it destiny. She talked fast, telling me she'd just moved over from across the Bay Bridge. Being as small as I was, that was a whole world away at the time. She was new and alien. A cool wind in the midst of the muggy atmosphere that was our fourth grade class.

We talked in a way kids usually didn't. She told me things about herself. How she'd felt about moving. How she felt about her parents, who had recently split. How much she loved sunsets, or those little flowers that made your chin glow yellow, and were undeniable proof that you liked butter when it did. I told her things about myself, too—things I hadn't known until I said them out loud. She made me brand new.

One morning she came to school and I could tell something was different. Her eyes looked tired. Her gaze wouldn't find mine. She was more interested in the shine of the laminated wooden desk in front of her. This pain wracked my chest and the feeling of a ball formed in my throat, which from then on I came to associate with love. I tried to grab hold of her hand. She pulled it away from me as if I were a hot stove she'd been told not to touch.

"What's wrong?"

She quietly shook her head back and forth.

"What's wrong?"

"Leave me alone."

She still wasn't meeting my eyes. We went on like this for most of the day. Tears welling up and being brushed away on both of our faces.

"Just tell me what I did wrong."

"My mom says we can't be friends."

It hit me at ninety miles per hour. It slammed into me like that kid who was just too eager to catch you while playing tag.

"She says we can't be friends," she repeated, "'cause I'm white and you're black. And that's not okay."

In retrospect, I wonder what made her mother feel that way. Was it a family thing, passed on from her own parents? A generational curse that she'd simply inherited? Had some African Americans she'd known in her past put a bad taste in her mouth about black folk? Or maybe it was for no apparent reason at all? Would it have changed if she had known me?

After getting off of work one afternoon and walking home, one of my best friends told me she was at the Noodles & Company that was on my way. She asked me to stop by. I walked in, minus my work shirt, which the heat had insisted I take off, wearing a wife beater and khaki pants. My hair being what many would've called nappy, thanks to the heat and humidity. I walked up to the table where three white women were seated, one of them being my best friend, the other two being her sorority sisters whom I knew very well. We didn't talk too long. I stood and joked with them as they smiled up at me. We made plans to get together for something my fraternity was hosting on campus later. We said our goodbyes and I walked out the door.

As I left, one of the waiters came up to their table and asked if I had bothered them, and if he needed to call somebody. They told me later they were all completely dumbfounded. Our interactions that day were "so normal," they said. They didn't understand what would've made him make that assumption. The one I was closest with told me later she'd never seen racism before that day (and I didn't have the heart to tell her this wasn't my first experience). But the guy probably didn't think he was being racist. He saw a black man, in a wife beater with a nappy 'fro, approach three white women at what seemed like random to him. And maybe he didn't see the way the three of us were getting along. Maybe he didn't notice their smiles or how relaxed we all were with each other. He saw what the rest of the world and the news had shown him was trouble. He probably was just trying to help. (He probably thought he was doing the right thing.)

LIKE HOME

MARY BIRNBAUM

In bed one night I said to the ceiling and my husband, "I really think we need to get an emergency plan together, in case there's an alien takeover." It was not a joke, but my husband laughed. His laughter stirred mixed emotions. First, I was sort of relieved. He was laughing because the possibility of alien invasion was so remote. But I was also irritated because I thought the laugh was edged with derision. And it came out of him, and I had a mild distaste for nearly everything about him. I turned over in bed to face the open window. A dry huff of Santa Ana wind blew in and chapped my eyes, so I shut them. The problem with my husband was that while he might be infuriating, I had decided I was going to need him during the invasion.

I'd had a dream that the world was on fire. Maybe alien fire, maybe wildfire; the origin was not explicit (and my fears are broad-ranging). In the dream, I loaded my two young daughters into the cab of my husband's Ford F-250 and trawled the smoldering hills of Earth looking for him. We encountered no humans until we found him in a deserted trailer park, alive among hollow shells of cars and homes. We rescued him, but the world was still so burnt I didn't know where to go next. Finding him on that barren Earth had been my only plan. When I woke up I wondered why my subconscious mind had thought to go after him at all.

It was brought to our attention that our next-door neighbor, Roger, hated us because of our inadvertent hospitality to a lot of gophers. The gophers had perforated the expanse of dirt surrounding our yellow house. The house was so run-down, so diminutive relative to the size of the lot, that we were essentially renting a quarter acre of sand. Our lean-to was like an afterthought. The land was dehydrated, uncombed, pocked with holes. A weed could scarcely thrive. We accepted the gophers as fixtures of an unkempt landscape. There was, after all, also a band of skunks roving the neighborhood, possibly raising a brood under our house. By "possibly" I mean that we regularly heard them skittering around below us in the crawlspace, and that they sprayed my dogs twice in a month. The second time they sprayed, the hit had been so acute that for a week just pulling up to the house was enough to make us gag. In Encinitas—for that was our city, and theirs—the skunks were notorious for appropriating space. Also, sometimes a brazen forty-pound raccoon tormented our dogs, holding ground, hissing loudly and stealing their food. Cone-faced opossums were standard fauna. Their sharp feet moved swiftly over a grid of fences like something from the circus. When you startled them, they'd swivel their heads toward you, black eyes beady and blank.

But it turns out that gophers are considered a blight, especially by neighbor Roger, who, the previous year, spent "one thousand dollars" hiring a squad of landscapers to rototill, fertilize, seed, and water the sand on his side of the fence. The lawn he cultivated was probably thirty-by-thirty feet, green, and rooted in what had become legitimate soil. It was shorn with the precision of a military barber.

Predictably, the rodents didn't honor the sanctity of a chain-link barrier. To our gophers, a rangy, resourceful population of tunnelers, Roger's side of the fence must have looked Edenic. Even I thought about chewing on that grass sometimes. Everything else in the Southern California was dry enough to snap, but that lawn was lush. Roger made sure of this, even though farmers in the Central Valley were watching their livelihood wilt in the heat and scarcity of the worst drought anyone in the state had ever seen, a symptom of warming on the global scale, brought on by irresponsible, shortsighted industrial water usage, but also by the type of Californian that Roger is. On furiously bright desert days, his sprinklers arced to and fro in steamy waves that cast prisms into the air.

Roger's stark green patch, his important investment, was being compromised by our negligence. He was moved to have a huge pile of fertilizer delivered to his home on the day of our daughter's fourth birthday party. I cannot accept that it was a coincidence. He must have seen the bounce house and dialed the manure depot in the same breath. On the morning of the party, I walked outside my home and my eyes welled up from the stench. I pulled my T-shirt over my nose and mouth. I went to the hardware store and bought bags of cedar mulch, in the hope that scattering it over my yard would make everything smell woodsy. But the shit always wins. Thirty children jumped all afternoon under a low-hanging dung haze. Roger was nowhere to be seen, though I imagined him just on the other side of his curtains, tittering in delight. On his lawn, the sprinklers said tick, tick, tick.

My husband was supposed to be a one-night stand, thirteen years ago, like all the other men I slept with during the period after a bad heartbreak. I'd been staggering around sad for a while when I recognized his car parked across the street from my mother's house. He was the nephew of the people across the street, in town from Kansas City. I saw his Buick station wagon and I knew I would find him inside his uncle's house, and that if memory served he would be above-average tall, sort of strapping and maybe game for a drink. My heart ached so bad that I was drunk when I was sober, but I was getting drunk a lot anyway. I didn't really know him, or hadn't known him since we were children and he came out to Encinitas for the summers. When I knocked on his uncle's door he was inside playing a video game. In those days, he wore striped polo shirts and low-slung cargo shorts and baseball caps with the names of Midwestern farm teams on them. He pulled the bill low over his blue eyes, so that he was always cocking his head up a little to see who he was talking to. He smelled like Dial soap.

He came out with me and we drank for hours and then we went back to the childhood home, where I was again living after college. He was in and out of my bed for a summer. Mostly in it. When he moved to Northern California to finish college, I decided to stuff my glove box full of books on CD and drive 900 miles alone to   surprise him. The drive started in the Southern California desert but thirteen hours later, the top of the same state could have been another planet. After ten hours on the I-5, I crossed to the coast on the 299, a two-hour course of switchbacks where oversized, hissing logging trucks careened like Formula 1 drivers. A dense stand of redwoods lurched up at the sky on one side, the opposite edge dropped into a thousand-foot ravine. I had made the long, lonely drive and I was still a person frayed at the edges by heartbreak, so maybe it makes sense that when I finally arrived at my boyfriend's dorm it felt like some kind of home. I stayed for a year. When he graduated we moved back to Encinitas and I thought about careers. None of them appealed very much. I thought about flying away from home, finally, alone, tapping some dream from childhood, heading for something exotic and unknown. But I didn't fly to any place. I let him get me pregnant. Then I agreed to marry him.

A little after my daughter was born, while the bank forced the sale of my childhood home (where my mother still lived), Mom's old black Lab began to die. Signs of Pony's decrepitude came in a cascade, leading up to the end. Like how every day he peed uncontrollably, prodigiously on the waxy hardwood floors before she could get him outside. The urine was acrid and even after Mom disinfected, the stench remained. Pony lost his appetite for McDonald's cheeseburgers. He couldn't muster strength to climb into the front seat of Mom's car. His eyes got milky and unseeing. Our rented house was close by, and I could daily find the two of them in the backyard, she on the phone with the bank, weeding vegetable plants (she made neat piles of the weeds on the pavers which sometimes did not get taken to a barrel, but decomposed over days where they lay scattered like ideas for punctuation) and Pony laying in the sun, black back gleaming, always as close as he could get to her feet.

One night I went to that house to check on my mom. I lugged my chubby baby, strapped down in her car seat like a dirigible barely tethered. Not finding my mother inside, I went around to the side yard. I passed through the gap in a hedge of night-blooming jasmine and found her lying on the bricks of the patio with Pony. The dog was alive yet, but barely. He was unable to move, so Mom lay alongside him on the ground because she wasn't strong enough to carry him anywhere.

As a child I'd always had the suspicion that I had the prettiest mother, a feeling which could have been linked to her general lighthearted-ness, her light-footedness, her smiling. There on the patio she was still the prettiest mother, but she'd gotten thinner with the stress of loss. She let grays rove all over her dyed brown hair and she had on an outfit I knew she'd worn for a couple days. A cigarette was burning itself out in an ashtray. Pony smelled of his own noxious excrement, of the decay emanating outward from his organs going stale, and of that unmistakable near-death smell for which I can't think of a better word. My mom was sniffling intermittently, not from the cold. It was an Olympics of suffering between the two of them on the frigid stone.

"I tried to make sure he knows I'm here by talking to him and petting him, but I think he's in pain. I don't know if he knows it's me." Mom's face was pressed against the patio bricks, her red nose six inches from the dog's black one.

"I think he might need to go to the vet," she said.

"Do you think they can help?" I asked.

"So he can die. But I don't think I can go."

I felt strongly that I also could not go. I was terrified. I started to try to figure out a compassionate way to extricate myself from the situation. I called my husband.

He arrived soon and offered to take Pony to be euthanized. I left the baby with my mother. I would drive the car so my husband could hold the sixty-pound dog on his lap on the passenger side. On the way, he gentled into Pony's ear about how we loved him and how he would be okay. The vet's office was deserted and clean and my husband lay Pony on an operating table while in low tones a kind young doctor described the procedure and its associated costs. Everything would be relatively quick and somewhat expensive.

"That's fine. I can pay."

I was surprised by my husband's offer. He could pay. Barely. Why would he pay? Likely because he knew my mom could not. So, maybe for her and how everything had really gone to shit for her. But probably for me.

The vet retrieved a set of syringes. Pony was inert and so was I, but my husband seemed comfortable in that room. It occurred to me then that he would have made a good vet. Any kind of doctor really, considering how collected he was under the exacting light, how he never shrank from the table but stood against it like he could belong there. I imagined his steady hand in a surgery, calm and useful over some vulnerable body. He hovered near Pony while the vet plunged the shots into that motionless black back. He said "good boy" to Pony softly over and over. Good boy. Good boy. I could think of nothing coherent to tell the dog, so I pressed my hand to one of his back legs, so he could feel I was there, and cried a little. When the injections were done the vet took the empty syringes and left us alone. I don't know how long it took for Pony's heart to stop. Minutes probably, but the room felt very still for a long time. Eventually he was gone, and the room was stiller. The vet said the body would be taken care of. That was included in the fee. We could stay as long as we needed, go home when we liked. On the ride home without Pony, I thought: remember this moment. How good he was and how you needed him. Think about this, the next time you think marriage is too hard.

After he helped Pony die, after strangers took possession of my childhood home and my mother moved to a condo the size of a dorm room, my husband started to take over most all the domestic minutiae at our house. The new baby required a lot of my time, and I let her have all of it. My spouse found joy in quotidian things, in automatic bill pay, regular oil changes and the copious, innovative use of bleach. He bought Ajax, not Comet, a brand preference I allowed myself to be bothered by, even though I could not be bothered to bleach any surface, brand notwithstanding. He went to work every day. He flew in and out of town on business. I noted arrivals and departures with only cursory interest, and gradually his routine included going to his buddy's house between work and home. He said he was working hard and he deserved to relax. His interest in fantasy sports and drinking with his friends seemed infantile to me, though it's true that I spent most of my twenties in a drunken stupor. It's even true that the night in 2004 when the Red Sox won the pennant I took the opportunity to shed my pants and panties and I ran hollering, bottomless in the streets, like a loose animal. I did similar versions of that activity for the whole long, blurry decade. But as I drank less (pregnancy, breastfeeding) and mothered more, I allowed myself to feel very virtuous and I addressed my husband's happy hour excursions with blazing reprobation. I became a world-class threat inventor, an artist of the empty ultimatum. (I will set all your clothes on fire, I will call your mother, I will leave you.) He fell into heavy drinking and stopped doing the dishes. Sometimes he didn't come home for several days on end.

And sometimes, particularly after we had a second daughter and he and I were still at our worst, I would let myself remember that moment of grace; I would try to conjure the man who was so merciful to my mom and her dog. But all I could recall was my own helplessness watching Pony die, the slowness of the minutes before I could flee.

When the house next door to my childhood home went up for sale recently, I wandered in, overly casual, during an open house. I knew I was just trying to sidle up to my old home in the only legitimate way I could. When I entered, the young realtor (slick button-down shirt tucked into his slacks, loafers, huge metal watch saying tick tick tick) was talking with a prospective buyer. The house was so small, she said, for the price. (The house was the exact footprint of my house that was not mine, just over the fence.) The realtor smiled and told her that the contractors had redone all the duct work, and that these were hardwood floors, not laminate like you find in so many flipped houses. I nodded, though not really part of the conversation between the realtor and the prospective buyer, nodded like I knew what a duct was. He said they took it right down to the studs to renovate and update it. That's what they call it when you reduce it to an empty frame: taking something down to the studs.

For months after the bank finally took Mom's house I had avoided driving down her street, which ran perpendicular to my own. One day, on a masochistic impulse, I found myself on Arden Drive, and where our sweet cottage had been there now stood a maze of sticks, in a vague embarrassing pattern that remembered faintly the rooms where we'd lived. The living room, the kitchen, the halls and my childhood bedroom were hollow space where a breeze now freely blew.

I met the couple who eventually bought the house next door. It was my mother's doing. Even though the bank had ousted her from the neighborhood and many of the neighbors regarded her now like someone fallen, she returned often, visiting people and searching like someone cheerful and lost. She was dyeing her hair regularly again. She was picking out cute outfits every day and accessorizing with flare. She told me she heard the next-door house had been bought by a nice young couple and that we should introduce ourselves. To her it did not seem odd to be the visiting strangers who used to live next door. I went because I wanted to know who it was who could afford to buy on our old street these days. The woman who answered the door was enormously pregnant and beautiful in a glowing way that made it difficult look right at her for too long. Her husband was absent, or more precisely he worked from a converted office in the back from which he rarely emerged. I asked where she had moved from and she said Las Vegas. She used to be a dancer in a circus there. *Of course you were*, I thought. I mused that I'd pay, too, to come and gawk. At our excited urging, she left the room to dig up a picture from an old circus program. She returned with a big glossy play-book and paged to the center to find herself. For her part in the show, she had been a bird. She wore a feathered mask. Her costume was full of floor-length plumes in brilliant hues. The feathers accentuated her body contours, shooting outward from a bodice in wild trajectories, in sprays of color. In the photo she was mid-leap. Her arms were flung out. Her powerful quadriceps muscles folded one over the other. Her head tilted back. Her eyes trained far above on something we couldn't see. She was a peacock and a phoenix and a parrot and a dove—all those creatures exotic and capable of imminent flight.

When it came to the moonscape of our yard, that is, the yard of my husband and myself and the wily gophers who darted in and out, without discussion we united against Roger. His lawn was preposterous, especially since it sprouted in front of a dwelling that was—like so many of the original structures in the neighborhood—a shambles of termite-eaten boards in need of paint or demolition. He was not friendly toward the kids. We knew he spoke unkindly about us to the other neighbors. He was as close to an enemy as we could contrive, and we needed one badly.

At some point, early on in living at the house, we had made half-hearted attempts to irrigate our yard. We watered in the spirit of possibility. We denied the desert. But when knowledge of Roger's acrimony became widespread, we brought all hydration to a halt. Whenever our dog, Wyatt, decided to chase gophers, sheets of dry dirt would billow up into the sky and descend slowly on our kids, our house, on Roger's lawn. Wyatt never caught a gopher and I, for one, wouldn't have liked to see that gore anyway. We had our bursting shack to attend to; our babies and dogs and arguments. Our nocturnal menagerie. Our drippy plumbing. Our unknowable ductwork.

The other night I lay with my five-year-old daughter while she fell asleep in my bed. The smell of night-blooming jasmine wafted in toward us through an open window. Even when covered in desert dust, jasmine is sweet and heady. The tiny blooms pop from the hedge like stars. My husband came in and stood close to the bed. He leaned down and reached for my face. We were not accustomed to touching one another anymore, so I receded away from him, down into the pillow. Still, he took my right earlobe in his fingers and loosed the earring there from its clasp. He set it on my daughter's bedside table. Then he did the same thing to the other ear. The studs clattered briefly together on the nightstand.

He said, "Aren't these hurting you?"

My husband is probably right that the hostile alien takeover is a long shot. Because the rational part of me (stick with me here) knows that, while the likelihood of extraterrestrial life is pretty high, chances are slim that aliens could ravage humans the way we wreck each other. We wreck each other and rebuild. We make each other over and over. And maybe under all that rubble, under the fertile ruin, there is a home.

SELF-PORTRAIT WITH CAT
DANIEL LUSK

As if a fool might give
a wise account of himself,
whose past is a patchwork
of regrets and non sequiturs

to whom every embrace was a gift
and every kiss a leaving.

There is no cat on the big red chair.

It is true, I have a mouth
for Irish whiskey and stomach
for the porridge of knowledge.
A heart for song and a wild eye for beauty

and desire, like the old anger, simmers still.

A white cat would be portentous.

Mother and father dead,
orphaned by my children,
family lore about some class of Indian,
the one thing certain of my heritage
is that I'm neither fish nor fowl.

And no longer waiting to be famous.

An old cat with tufted ears seems right,
sleepy there against a pillow, sanguine.

There is my farmer neighbor, Boone,
alighting from the school bus, face and hands
bloodied, as if a barn cat had attacked him
for sitting on its tail at tea.

He had been trying a new approach
to the high jump called the forward roll

over barbed-wire fences in the field.
What of a barn cat out of the feral Marn,
who fled forlorn alleys of London in a grim century?

Fifty years ago I was awakened quaking
from fitful sleep in a stone pension
across the street from the church
of St. Sebastian in Salzburg
by the soul-sundering *wrong* and again
wrong of a massive bell that began the clang
and chime of bells across the entire city
their Matins calls.

There hangs the haunting, life-sized,
painted wooden Madonna,
ten-inch hilt of a dagger protruding
from the top of one bleeding breast
in company of the agonizing Christ
with his mocking crown of thorns.

Would that the cat were Ozymandias,
King of Cats in his morning coat and cravat.

What did I write then I cannot now
—that long-ago singing to that long-ago girl
and who was she to ignite my song?

Come back now: the hillside, the copse
of trees, the summer rain
and herself, eager as I was and almost
as young—loving what we did and didn't do

until she got up and ran, taking her name
with her. What difference would it make
if this were true? Such love
needs neither names nor bed,
a holly bush to hang a garment on will do.

Loss is the bed we learned to lie upon.
Remember the pebbles soft as kisses
against your windows, the stones
hard as unbridled desire at your door.

I've seen my words in print and paint,
in hammered copper, cut into steel,
yet recall them not at all. They've gone
like the cat who might have been.

COURT OF COMMON PLEAS

DIONNE CUSTER EDWARDS

The carpet on the fourth floor of the courthouse building spits a stench of bitterness, stale air full of a kind of fragile ache and wicked concoction of rips and slivers, ashes and fragments, broken lives. The elevator pours us out the double doors, the suits and casuals. Like mice, we scatter in the light, hands full of folders full of affidavits—people negotiating freedom, financial support, holidays and weekends, so many troubles and bodies in one big room.

In domestic court there are few families intact. We are blood and samples, sad stories, temporary orders, people on opposite sides. Stuck in a system that serves law and wounds the same careless seasoning of obstacles and disregard. We are children, parents, caregivers, reduced to edicts and orders, and a magistrate in a hurry to move on to the next shutter and bone.

We are all waiting for judgment. For someone to see you missing another day of work. Pleading with the judge to see you for more than just conflicts and thorns. We are plaintiffs and defendants, whispers and screams. Piles of paternity, custody, child support cases on the court docket, plenty of rope to hang us all. Our messy lives plucked and hung for the public to consume, each of us stuck, foolish, or toting a bit of chagrin.

I was all three of those things. He was drunk the night I met him (and on some mornings in court). Idle and alone, he leaned on the barstool in the corner, watched me move about the crowded room. I ignored him until he found a way to meet me. He had a sloppy charm—wrote some pleading nonsense on a paper napkin. I had a list of objections—just enough pity and politeness, and not enough will. I was ready to leave, alone, and I did—but not without giving him a way to reach me. He was bold, persistent, and sad—like fruit skin, bruised, and worm-holed. I knew better then, and now.

Until you make choices, color your own messy life, you do not know the bow in the rope, how low it hangs, how heavy it bends towards the floor—

how desperate it feels to love someone so much you tug on their small limbs. How your life is a dripping faucet of court dates, hours away from work, fees, spar and differing. How we are two strangers who have a son together. How neither of us discusses the soiled details with him or each other. How together and separate, we both try to protect him from our decisions, the back and forth of storms.

After more than ten years in court, on and off and a few breaks in between, we stand in front of this bench mapping our mistakes. We are on either side of a desperate line between fear and enabling, a crooked bend in the air between us. He wants reassurance, and control. I want freedom, and control. We both want time with our son. We want in contrast, some of the same things at the same time. We sing our plea of blame and equal. The judge entertained by our urgency and conflict, by our desire to be needed or left alone. In court, we exhaust all the ways to file judgments and motions that explain how much we both love our son—but there is no way to love him here.

BIRDS, BEES

TA'RIQ FISHER

Now let me tell you something about messing with white women, my moms said.

Always started her lectures like that, *now let me tell you. Now let me tell you* about staying out after dark, *let me tell you* about managing your money, *let me tell you* how to wash your clothes and iron them with a spritz of starch and fold them crisp— not that way, do it like this, like me—how to make breakfast for dinner in a pinch, how to rub tea tree oil on your scalp and wrap the durag tight so you wake up with your waves looking right in the morning. She said it like, class is in session, sit down and let me learn you. When she was ready to let me tell you, whether it was me or my little brother or my older sister, we'd roll our eyes and get the notebooks out in our heads and prep for her to talk until our ears got stale and could just about fall off.

You know they don't understand black folks, she said, wagging a finger with her voice. You might think it's all fun and games right now, having some white girl on your arm, but she'll grow up one day and you might not be ready for what that brings. You only nineteen—too young to be doing so much, getting all serious. Don't let no white girl get you caught up.

I was sitting on our living room couch. It was an old couch, leather, hot in the summer and grabby with skin, so I had to hold out my arms a bit to avoid getting sweat-stuck. DC's heat wave had made it feel like the eye on a stove. The couch was a mainstay, been here through renovations and remodels, before my moms had itchy carpet installed and after that same car-pet got ripped up and out after we stained it too much. I'd come to know this couch all too well; for more than a decade straight it's been her favorite place to let me tell you. Adjacent to each arm of the couch were tall potted plants that my moms would replace whenever they overgrew, since we didn't bother to avoid stepping on the dead leaves. Healthy, the plants had waxy leaves that made them look fake, but I bit into one once when I was younger (for scientific purposes) and tasted the real thing.

Don't look at the plants when I'm talking to you boy, my moms carped. Always everywhere but where you supposed to be, just like your brother.

I looked at her face. She had the smoothest face, like you could dip a hand into her cheeks and watch them ripple. Served her well for swapping personalities: she could go from lunatic-mad to pleasant and lukewarm like she had woken up with the face ironed right on, wrinkle-free. But right then, cutting into me with her gaze, her face was just short of *I'm ready to cuss you the fuck out.*

Couple of hours ago she found a condom on my dresser, her hawk eyes skimming past the loose change scattered about, past the lotion and deodorant and glass vessels of cologne, locking right on to the glossy gold square that conjures dread within the heart of every parent that had skirted past the talk. (Our talk—if you could call it that—came about when I was about fourteen, after she noticed that I had been locking my bedroom door more often. One random morning soon after, she knocked on my door, calling me down for breakfast, and when I got downstairs she had a fresh banana and a butter knife sitting on one of our good plates. One bruised, mangled, traumatized banana later, I had gotten the talk—her version of it, at least. What it amounted to: If you don't want your penis turning inside out like this banana, you better keep it in your pants.) When I came home, she didn't mince words. You been having sex? she asked, crinkling the condom in her hand as she held it in front of me. Couldn't hide the look of mortal surprise on my face, so I fessed up: Yeah. I have.

That landed me right on the family couch, getting a verbal ass whooping of three lectures in rapid succession. The Do's and Don'ts (what you should do: don't), yet another rendition of *I Ain't Raising No Babies*, and of course, the Possible Perils of Messing with White Women.

Tekelle, who stayed instigating like a younger sister instead of the older one she was, bounded downstairs, giggling, ready to chime in because she had her fill of eavesdropping. My moms, her nose scrunching like she had just caught a whiff of trouble, turned her back to both of us and leaned against the window to watch the street.

It must be rough being with a white girl, Tekelle said. Do they even put lotion on? You ever seen a white girl that ain't have ashy feet?

If Allison—known in my family as That White Girl—was here, she'd look down at her feet right about now. Sometimes I'd catch her without socks on, grabbing one of her ankles and bringing her foot up close for an inspection, and I'd always see the ashy crevices on her heel and feel the roughness of her skin against my hand. Moments like that, I'd shake my head and say, Cocoa butter ain't but ninety-nine cents for one of those big-ass bottles. But I guess she liked having pieces of sandpaper for feet because she never listened and she never learned.

Shut up, Tekelle, I quipped, remembering the time Allison and I were wrapped up in bed once, her asking me, Why're your feet so soft? and me wanting to say, Why aren't yours?

Tekelle had her hands up in the air (don't shoot!) and her elbows flared out. She had been twisting her hair up, so the left half of her hair was in tendrilled ropes that came down to her shoulder while the right half was still 4A-kinky and tumbled into half an afro. When she came near me I could smell the products: the shea butter, the leave-in conditioner, the two-in-one that she had put in to loosen her hair up, and that rotten nutty stench of coconut oil, fresh out the cooking aisle. I turned my face up and gave her a shitty look.

That mess stinks, I said.

Don't be mad at me because you fine with having dry hair, she said.

Oh, you natural now so you neo-soul, right? Black soap and Erykah Badu, right? *You need to pick yo' afro daddy,* I sang in my throaty Erykah voice.

Tekelle rolled her eyes and went into the kitchen to wet her hair in the sink. I looked back at my moms, who was holding a handful of curtain and peering out into the street, that marigold sunset lathering her skin. Something was off; only time my moms stopped in the middle of her lectures was if something was going down, or she was about to make something go down.

Ma, you alright? I said.

The sun almost down, she said. Where your brother at?

Couldn't find Darius at his usual places, not at the ninety-nine-cent store blowing dollar bills on sour gummy worms and off-brand oatmeal cream pies to satisfy his sweet tooth, not at Walton's trying to bum some extra mambo sauce for his wings, not at the asphalt basketball courts, not riding his dirt bike down Q Street like he was one of them boys from Baltimore. Thought he might have been out selling tree to the cats that lived around Columbia Heights, but I had checked his room before my moms rushed me out the door and all the weed was still there in the shoebox under his bed.

Being older, I was automatically delegated my brother's keeper--hunter, more like—to round him up before my moms tried to break a foot off in his ass. With shoes on he had two inches on me, stood six-foot-three at only sixteen years old, towering over my moms and Tekelle—but my moms told him like she told me whenever I slipped up and happened to mean-mug her the wrong way, I don't care if you six-ten, I'll get on a chair and beat your ass if I have to. But after two kids and hundreds of decibels of sound wasted away, after all that monstrous energy spent deep-yelling and cussing and   carrying on, she had tried to adopt a more diplomatic parenting policy the third time around. She was by far the most lenient with Darius, and he made sure to take advantage of that.

Darius was the worst of what I remember of our dad and somehow equal and opposite our moms; usually he was compassionate and exuded her image, but it didn't take much to bring out our dad's angry, acidic, smart-ass mouth. My moms was a careful woman, like all the matriarchs of our family: in the same way as her moms and grandmoms before her, she locked most of her humanity away for the sake of being strong, because families like ours—broken-frame fuckups—demanded a practical woman that knew how to be both mommy and daddy (because daddy don't come around no more), a   multitasker who could be tender yet stern with a backhand to match. But Darius had a penchant for pushing his luck, sometimes when you'd least expect it. He straddled the line between angel and asshole like a leaf doing a turnover in the wind, shifting in the blink of an eye.

The sky was creeping up on that blue part of nighttime on our dilapidated block of Southeast, and there were dim cones of orange everywhere, street lights pushing out as much power as they could to keep the dark away. I was sitting on the steps that led out of our cramped townhouse, half because I wanted some air on my skin, half because my moms wouldn't accept me walking into the house without my brother in tow.

The heat must've driven everyone outside (because don't nobody here have no damn working AC). Next door neighbor, Mr. Johnson, an old man with a ballooned belly that spilled over his belt buckle, was in his yard in a tank-top and jean shorts, shuffling around in his slippers, tending to his rusty blue birdhouse and sticking his hands beneath his waistband to scratch. There was enough space in front of the apartment complex across the street from us—my moms called it Projects 'R' Us—for grass to run around in, and everybody's kid over there was doing just that. The moms were close, gossiping about whatever women gossip about, trash-ass men or something, and occasionally stopped to snap their fingers at one of the kids and give them a look, *Don't make me come over there and light your yellow ass up.* Even at nineteen I still got that look—hell, even at twenty-two Tekelle still got it, like her helping with the bills didn't matter if she came too slick out the mouth. Who I assumed were the fathers of the kids were gathered around a couple of cars parked on their side of the street, smoking weed and bumping oldies, laughing their deep laughs. I was enjoying the smell of their weed when my little brother came back, cradling something wrapped in a blanket.

Michael? he said, like I was long lost or something.

D, is that a baby? I asked, dismissing his lateness.

Yup, it's a baby. I got a white girl pregnant and she's coming to live with us, he scoffed.

He walked over and motioned for me to uncover the bundle he was swaddling. I pulled the blanket back and an ash-gray bullmastiff puppy's eyes opened and widened at the sight of me. Its eyes were a vibrant, cool blue, like a glacier had melted over its pupils. It bit the air twice and tried inching its way out of my brother's arms, coming for me like a gray baby searching for a nipple. He dropped it into my arms and at first I tried holding it like I held Darius when he was a baby, but then I thought about how Darius used to spit-up on me like he knew what he was doing, so I put my hands on the sides of it and held it at arm's length, letting the blanket fall to the grass. Even in half-darkness I could spot her features.

Hey, little girl, I said in my best babying voice. Don't you go spitting up on me.

She radiated heat and seemed content to rest with my hands on her sides, swaying her hind legs along with the gusts of wind that came by. She wasn't wearing a collar.

Does this thing have all its shots? I said, thinking of worms getting under my skin.

Ain't have time to go to the vet when I saved it from dying on the side of the damn road.

I shot him a look.

We can take her to the vet tomorrow, he said.

Where she supposed to sleep?

Let me and moms figure that out.

I laughed without realizing at first. The thought of my moms letting something into her house that would lick its own ass and not offer to pay any bills brought a smile to my face.

Moms about to have her put down by dinner, I said.

Don't you got a white girl to be playing plantation with? he retorted.

He put a hand to his brow and started turning in circles, scanning the street in front of us. Oh look, captain! A ho! he said, pointing at nothing with one hand and tapping my shoulder with the other. Go save her!

Don't get hit, nigga, I warned.

The front door opened behind us. Of course I had to be holding the damn dog.

The hell is that, Michael? my moms said.

Tekelle was over her shoulder talking that shit: Oh, I know you not trying to bring no dog in here.

Shut up, Tekelle, Darius quipped.

She's mine, I said without thinking. I'm the one that's going to be paying for everything anyway.

I pulled the dog closer to me and held her the same way I held pre-spit-up Darius.

We kind of stood there looking stupid and stayed quiet for a minute. I shifted my weight between each foot and Tekelle put her hands on her hips, then crossed her arms. Darius stood there, staring at my moms, who was giving him back every look he gave her. The dog didn't bark, as if she knew that this was just how the big conversations went in our family.

I had a Rottweiler when I lived with y'all's great-grandfather in Waldorf, my moms said finally.

She might as well have said, *Now let me tell you*, y'all own that dog, y'all take care of it and feed it, put a damn sweater on it if you want; I don't want nothing to do with it, and I better not catch it shitting on my floors or I'll shit on yours.

Felt my chest getting warm, then wet, then warm again. Looked down and turned my nose up in the air once I caught a whiff. She had peed on me. Tekelle cackled over my moms's shoulder.

Better get to training, my moms said, chuckling as she closed the door behind her.

For the weeks she went without a name, I stuck close to her and watched how she behaved, how she sniffed the ground and took quick to getting house-broken, almost like she knew my moms wasn't playing around. Accidents became rare once she got used to being in the house, and she liked to be outside enough that she usually took care of business out front in our little patch of yard.

Named her Hera because of the way she walked with her dog-chest out, trotting around with footsteps that only got heavier and more well-placed, regal almost, like we weren't anything to her but subjects. She reminded me of a pit bull named Zeus that Mr. Johnson used to have. Hera walked like him: strong, pushing the world off her feet. When he was alive, Zeus didn't bark much, not even at the other dogs that would be chained up in front of the apartments across the street. And he listened to Mr. Johnson most of the time—a far cry from Hera. I called out Hera! the same way Mr. Johnson used to call out Zeus! and she would stop what she was doing and consider if she wanted to listen. I got a kick out of that.

Only time she got out of hand was when someone new got too close, too fast. Even as a teething puppy she could put a hurt on someone, her newborn teeth still potent enough to tear flesh. I knew when the play nips turned into bites. One day a friend of my moms's came through to drop off a pan of food and tried to play with Hera, but Hera wasn't having one bit of it. She went ballistic, nothing but loud barks and deep growls and bared teeth and wide eyes, *I'll fuck you up* eyes. Had to flick her nose and bring out my grown man voice, then try to distract her with the piece of ham I had left in the micro-wave. She clamped down on the ham, sat by my moms's I-just-got-home-don't-talk-to-me chair, and fell asleep.

Her weight shot up over time, seemed like she got bigger after each bowl. Got to that stage where she didn't know her own size after a few months. Her paws got close to the size of my fists, and when she'd stand up to balance her front paws on my chest and give me those You're home! licks, she almost always knocked a pocket of air out of me. And she was a slobbery dog, like all dogs with heavy flews like hers, letting saliva pool in her mouth until it dripped everywhere, so I had to repurpose some old washcloths into spit rags and went through them like tissues each time she got to drooling.

She put a serious dent in my net worth, but the money I'd been saving up from my job at the shoe store wasn't doing anything but sitting in an account anyway. I'd been trying to save up about half a year of rent to prep for when I finally moved out of my moms's place, a day I couldn't quite imagine but knew would come anyway, but Hera postponed Moving Day to who knows when. Didn't mind any of it though, not the money I took out of my savings for shots and food and toys, not the double shifts I had to work to recoup some of my losses, nothing. Waking up in my bed with Hera next to me made me realize that my moms wasn't only cutting Darius some slack—she was cutting me some, too.

Allison stirred out of her sleep when I woke up moving my shoulders in time with whoever was outside blasting Drake out of some real quality speakers. Her neighborhood was in the mostly white, upper-class part of metropolitan DC, but black people still rolled through to get across town and they were the only ones playing music that loud. Thought it added some life to her neighborhood—swear I could hear mosquitos fucking on the tree outside her place, it was that quiet. She couldn't even be mad, really, but she acted like it.

Who the fuck is playing music this early? she huffed, rolling her naked ass off me.

I wanna see you do more in this life if we takin' it there, I rapped along, locking eyes with Allison, pointing and bending my fingers like I was in a music video.

Stop, she said, clearly unamused.

No—I stopped myself, still shoulder-leaning side to side.

I was about to say *No nigga*, but a couple of months ago, when I was rapping along to a song that said *nigga* as a verb, pronoun, modifier, and adjective all in the same line, she got real uncomfortable in the face and told me she didn't like me saying that. Almost took offense, but then I remembered that this—us—was still relatively new to her. For most of her life she was used to boys that turned ripe red after being in the sun too long. (I was used to girls that put lotion on before they stepped outside.)

When Drake's voice started to dopple away, she gripped my shoulders and kissed me to keep me from moving, and once she had me pulled close and caught, cradling my neck in the bend of her arm, she fingered through my hair with her free hand and let out laughs of air through her nose.

Our kids would have the wildest hair, she said. Brushing is going to be tough.

I laughed. In my head I pictured two or three little coffee-cream mixtures of us sporting knotty-ass hair that could snap a comb in half if it ventured too deep.

You don't brush that type of hair, I said as gently as I could. Not your kind of brush.

Then what do you do?

Take a wide-tooth comb through it on wash days.

Wash day? she said with eyes that looked like she was taking notes. How often is that?

Once a week, maybe twice, I said.

She looked disgusted, like I had spit in her mouth (when she wasn't ready). Then shook her head like she was never-minding her follow-up questions.

I'm still coming over on the Fourth, right? she asked.

I nodded. This year her parents would be spending the Fourth at their beach house in Virginia to gawk at fresh scenery and try to bring some spark back to their marriage. Not wanting Allison to be alone, I invited her over. My moms had simmered down with time and didn't mind her presence—though she'd have a meltdown for the ages if she found out how often I snuck Allison into my room and cupped a hand over her mouth while we fucked.

You'll get to spend some more time with Hera, I said.

Her eyebrows almost touched when she frowned.

I don't think she likes me, she said. Maybe she can tell I don't like dogs.

Hera, I said as reassuringly as I could manage, is part of the family.

Am I part of the family?

She shivered a bit like she had caught something up her spine, probably nervous from all the bullshit in that loaded-ass question. Took me a minute of unfilled silence to think of a loaded counter.

Do you want to be? I asked. I mean, in the future, one day—maybe.

I always tell you I can see us married. You know, our kids would be beautiful, she said through a yawn, settling her face in my neck.

The way she said it wasn't matter-of-fact or inevitability; the way she said it, the way her tone went from high to low and back again, almost made it sound like she was asking a question. Our creamy little mulatto kids would be pretty, right?

Allison and I started out as anything but serious. We pushed our faces together at a party when we were drunk, but I didn't think it would grow into much more than that. Both of us had our fair share of relationships and hookups, but whenever we had time to meet up and hang, it was electric. And you know what they say about attraction. Before I could realize it, we got close, got intimate and attached and started treading serious waters. Forces at work, I guess.

Never really thought I would end up with a white girl, but Allison had a body like a black girl, which was exciting in the way that someone from California tastes DC snowfall on their tongue for the first time: you can't help but want more. The white girls who looked like black girls, we called them snow bunnies, maybe because niggas seemed to go for them when it was cold out. Allison looked like one of those snow bunnies that would call me a nigger during sex, when it gets rough and neither of us are particularly thinking straight. Before she dyed it her hair was sandy blonde, but now it was a fresh-off-the-coals black that really made the green of her eyes pop. And even though she looked the part, she wouldn't dare call me a nigger or any variation of it. Wasn't so sure about her parents.

My first time meeting them, I was dressed sharp to the nines, went so far as to wear a fucking tie. When they first got sight of me, my fresh shape up and fade down the back, it was something out of a movie: the looks on their faces said Shit, paused, then went to, Oh…*shit*. Blinked so much during dinner I could swear they were flashing Morse code. S-O-fucking-S.

Her dad, an executive who worked near the Capitol, faithfully voted Republican like his life depended on it (if you think about it, it kind of did), and her moms, even though she dabbled in red and blue and had time to watch the news and deliberate since she worked from home three days a week, would stick her size-six foot down your throat if you said anything that resembled being pro-choice. The ultra-Christian in her wasn't having it, kind of like my moms when I tried to explain to her that sometimes I didn't feel like God was the kind of person-place-or-thing everyone thought He was. Allison's parents gave off *that* vibe: expert in all things Americana, opinionated bumper stickers and the like.

Allison was a blue-bleeding liberal, about as far left as you could get without veering into communism. The passion she had about politics gave her a restless look when she started yammering about checks and balances and landmark court cases, like she was already there in her office with the door marked SENATOR, pushing papers and filling out forms and meeting constituents and soaking up the bureaucracy and *loving* it all to hell and back. Made sense that she was at odds with her parents more often than not, Allison being the perfect model of rebellion. Always wondered how strong the bond was that tethered them together. The way I saw them interact, it was like gravity: them pulling her close, her pushing them back.

Don't ask me why, but sometimes I felt like she was doing me as a way of getting back at her parents. Like every time she swallowed, every time I had her grabbing her ankles or had her bent and twisted half-backwards she was saying *Fuck both of you!* in her head. But somewhere along the way I guess feelings started to surface; she brought up marriage more and tested my thoughts about kids. The way I saw it, if anything serious were to happen with us, it would be one of those milestone moments that, moving forward, changed everything. A line that, once crossed, warped our vision to see only the truest of colors. That's the scary thing though. You can never tell the person inside from the person out, what they're seriously thinking; all you can do is best-guess and hope that words line up with actions. But that's just how it goes. Forces at work, I guess.

The strip of apartments and townhouses on Minnesota Avenue were gearing up for the next stretch of summer. The Fourth was tomorrow, coming up on the peak of grilling season. I could smell it in the air. Mr. Johnson rolled his grill out of his basement and started hosing it down in his front yard. The younger people in the apartments across the street were playing music all day, putting on repeat the summer classics everyone always played at the family cookouts that made your aunt pull you out of your seat to two-step. Whoever was on the street bumping the music out of their car was mixing old school with new and I wasn't complaining.

I loved the resurgence of grilling season, when the spirit of the Fourth starts settling in and everyone gets patriotic enough to get some napkins and plates with stars and stripes on them. Made me feel like a kid again, when our grandmoms would take us on camping trips deep in Virginia every Fourth and throw all types of food on the grill. Our strip smelled like charcoal and meat smoke about ten hours out of the day—someone, somewhere close by was always having a kickback, grilling chicken and corn and taking turns tossing horseshoes in whatever yard space they had. And around peak grilling season the honeys on the block would start getting creative and carefree, wearing those short-shorts that left about this much to the imagination and those custom-made hoop earrings with their names in the middle.

After Mr. Johnson cleaned his grill, he kicked back in one of those adjustable lawn chairs and soaked up the rays, watching cars squeeze through our packed, double-parked street. I was outside with Allison and Hera, who was only in the mood to be just enough out of the shade to feel some heat against the back of her ears. She was picking at some of the grass, eager to dig it up. When her hands weren't stroking the fur on Hera's back, Allison was pushing a finger against Hera's lips while she nipped at the grass and laughed when Hera would give off a soft growl in protest. Could tell Allison and Hera were beginning to get along nicely.

Tekelle came outside, itching to be in somebody's business.

Well ain't you two just picture perfect, Tekelle said.

What the fuck you want Tekelle?

Don't nobody want nothing from you, stupid! You know niggas about to start shooting soon. I just want to enjoy what's left of the day.

Around the Fourth, New Year's, and sometimes on Christmas, the whole neighborhood would duck into hiding when daylight grew distant. We all knew what was coming. Music got turned down low so no one paid attention to it when someone turned it off. The chatting and kee-keeing would hush and people would say their goodbyes: Oh, alright now, it's about time for us to get going, got to put this boy down to bed before he's up all half the night. Before we got big enough to take care of ourselves, my moms would always *let me tell you* when the holidays came up, because the boys on the block liked to shoot off rounds to say, Congrats, we made it this far.

Shooting? Allison asked with no effort to mask her concern.

Niggas just like to play too much, Tekelle said. They ain't about to do nothing to your pretty little head.

Don't worry about it, I interjected. They don't shoot at nobody. Usually.

Like everything that goes down when you're least expecting it, it happened too quick to stop. For a second I could see Hera's gums and a snap of her white teeth gunning for Allison's hand and pulling back. Then drops of blood dotted the grass and Allison gave a wide-mouth-open scream that still rang in the air a second after she was done. I took Hera by her collar and led her inside—she was trotting along like she was the one taking me inside. The first aid kit we kept in the drawer under the kitchen knife set was enough to squeeze some gauze in the wound and wrap it in breathable bandages. Allison's hand wasn't gushing but it was red and mangled enough to where she had to hold it together to keep the fold of split skin in place, Hera had gotten her right in the webbing between her thumb and index finger. Without her other hand's intervention that skin probably would've waved in the breeze like a flag.

I'm okay, really, she insisted. I only screamed because she scared me. I think I pushed against her tooth.

The gauze around her hand already had a soaked-red bullseye staining it.

I don't know what got into her, I said.

Guess I should get this checked out, she said casually.

While I was driving her to the emergency room, her face went pale and it looked like sweat had settled on her skin, like the shock of what happened had finally dawned upon her. Or maybe the thinness of her nonchalance had worn off and she couldn't help being anything but serious. And maybe she was thinking serious things.

I can take care of this, okay? I reassured. I can take care of it.

Resting her forehead against the window, she closed her eyes and went *Mhm.* Couldn't figure out if she was dismissing my reassurance or dismissing me altogether.

The Fourth finally arrived. Rays of sunlight were cutting through the clouds, plumes of meat smoke wafting through the air, commotion at every corner. Seemed like everyone was coming outside to gossip and make space for grills. The block had just got to bumping the cookout music (even the kids were belting out *I wanna make sure I'm right girl, before I let go*) when a voice yelled out Twelve! and everybody dipped the next moment. Music record-scratched off, the moms took the kids inside, the men that were rolling joints on the hoods of cars swiped everything to the grass and scattered. Only reason we didn't hustle the fuck out of there along with them and get with the fucking program was because twelve had rolled up on *us*, and where do you hide when you're hiding from something whose superpower in life is to seek?

The hold my moms had on the front door made her look like she could rip it right off if she moved an inch—she wasn't going *anywhere.* Probably a good thing since Hera was inside with Tekelle barking her fucking brains out. Allison, with her now-stitched hand, still came over for the Fourth—and I'm sure she was regretting it. She stepped back in the grass and tried to take me with her, but I was more focused on Darius in front of me. Saw that leaf turning over in the wind.

The squad car's door popped open and out came one of DC's finest with his hand on his holster, trigger finger knuckle jutting out further from the rest. Dude had a bald head and a stern-cut face and cooped his eyes behind sunglasses, the whole vibe he was giving off warning us: *Don't.* But clearly he ain't never met my little brother.

Don't y'all pig ass niggas got nothing better to do than stirring shit up? Darius said, standing a few yards from where the cop had pulled up. It's a fucking holiday.

I'd seen him get like that before. Kind of like my moms when she swapped moods, but worse. His shoulders were squared back and the cords of his neck were pushed up against his skin, and though he started to take a few steps back, I realized quick that he was just giving himself more room. Then I saw that his hands had already begun to form fists, and my heart got to knocking around in my chest like my body was playing pinball.

D! I shouted, careful not to raise my voice too much. Come here.

What you want with us? Darius said to the cop.

Shut up, the cop said with bass in his voice. Get on the ground.

Fuck you, Darius snapped back.

D—that was all I could choke out. Before I knew it the words were caught in my throat, wrapped up with the next breath I had planned to take. My hands were sweating and it wasn't because of the heat.

Barely a second passed when the cop yelled Get on the ground! again and brought out his Glock. Then the whole world seemed to go stiff. My mom stood at the door, looking like she'd be right at home in a wax museum. Allison probably had some look of dread, but I couldn't turn around to find out. Darius looked like he was about to bolt like a spooked cat. If I could've seen Hera, there'd probably be droplets of drool suspended in the air around her from barking, those chops of hers flapping because she always had so much to say. And Tekelle, probably looking like she don't have nothing on her mind, like always. Bet if I had looked up to the clouds there'd be a flock of birds frozen in place, their wings spread, scanning as far and wide as their eyes could see, so wholly unconcerned with the chaos unfolding beneath them. Or maybe they'd be looking down at us, glancing to acknowledge our existence for one brief moment, then going about their own.

Hold up, I croaked when I realized time hadn't stopped at all, that the Glock was still aimed at my baby brother and I was yearning to say something, anything. He ain't do nothing.

Don't you fucking move.

Darius took a step back and looked like he was about to raise his hands, but the cop closed the gap between them and collided into him with a left hook that had the full support of his weight behind it. Clocked Darius right in his mouth, I heard the impact and it sounded like the something popped. They went to the ground like two alley cats, the cop still whaling on my baby brother.

My parents, Allison said shakily.

Could make out the red vessels in the whites of her eyes, they were that wide. The look on her face: eyes like dotted cue balls, raised brows that wrinkled her forehead and seemed to hang over the rest of her. She looked like a kid at the mall that had gotten away from her moms and couldn't see anything but the strangeness of being lost.

My parents called the cops.

Before I could ask why, Darius was on the ground with a knee on his back, staining the grass with his blood. My moms came down from the top steps with the roughest look I had ever seen on her and couldn't manage to get the words out to make sense of it all. That was when I realized she had been crying out the entire time, yelling for the cop to stop. When she got within a yard of the two of them the cop pointed his pistol at her face just as plainly as he would point a finger and she took a few frantic steps back, got down on all fours and started speaking to Darius, Just calm down baby, please, it'll be alright, I won't let nothing happen to you. Darius was gurgling, part like he was having trouble swallowing the blood in his mouth, part like he wanted to bawl but was going to hold it in if it meant doing it in front of others.

They stuffed Darius in the back of the squad car like luggage. Once we could go, me, Tekelle and my moms drove up to the station and stayed there until they stopped questioning him. Wasn't paying much attention to what was going on because I couldn't stop playing those last few hours back in my head.

The cop had waved his gun around like he was a conductor and directed us all to the ground, said if any of us moved, he'd shoot. Hera wouldn't shut the fuck up; that clearly made him nervous. Keeping us under the oversight of his Glock, he radioed for backup and two more squad cars pulled up a few minutes later, along with an Animal Control van. My daughter's inside, my moms repeated out loud to anyone that would listen. Just let me talk to her. She shouted Tekelle's name, told her to come to the door, to put her hands up and do as they said. A couple of cops put me, Allison, and my moms in cuffs, then went inside. I breathed a bit when they pushed open the door and called out to Tekelle. Part of me had heard a pop ripple through the air and saw my sister's blood spilling out into a flat red lake around her body—but then I heard Tekelle's voice and pushed those thoughts down to where I couldn't see them. She was holding Hera back, who was barking like she was trying to conjure up a storm. That's when Animal Control stepped up, tied the noose of a snare pole around Hera's neck, put her in the van. My vision was wet.

When we were all cuffed and flat on our stomachs, some of the cops went inside and started searching the house. Then the cop that had decked Darius lifted him to his feet and led him to the squad car, blood drying dark on his mouth. Allison, still lost in her eyes, turned to me.

Michael, she said, I'm sorry.

For what?

Yesterday I came home with the bite, she stammered, and my parents wanted to know where I got it from. So I told them. We started arguing because they cancelled their trip and said they were going to call the police—I said not to, Michael, I told them no—and I thought I convinced them, but— she left her mouth open as she trailed off. But they called anyway.

There was too much pounding going on in my head so I just looked at her for a while, then rolled my neck the other way and looked at the grass, the street, the faint sight of heads peering out of windows. Then my vision went wet again.

They uncuffed us about an hour later, after they had us chasing the edge of a circle with their questioning and tore through the house looking for a gun. Allison's parents told a hell of a tale, apparently. (Why? Not to be a nihilist but, it doesn't matter. Wouldn't matter in this life or any other life like mine, if the world had its way.) Tekelle walked wearily to the steps and sat down. Once my moms had the strength, she sat next to Tekelle on the steps and they leaned on each other and cried.

I'll fix this, Michael, Allison said. I'm going to do everything I can to fix this.

The cynic in me wanted to ask how—so I did. She said she didn't know yet, and her eyes scanned the grass as if the earth could give her a clue. I lightened up, told her I wasn't expecting an answer anyway. Some questions in life weren't ever formed with answers in mind.

Do you hate me? she said with misty eyes I had seen only a handful of times, when we had gotten into the worst of the worst of our fights.

No, I said. You can't change your parents.

She brought her hand over her mouth and whimpered, then wiped the tears off her face. I watched her do it, watched her shoulders jerk as she cried into her hand.

Do you hate them? I said.

I don't understand them, she said through gritted teeth. Am I supposed to?

Felt like forever was smashed into one breath, in, out. Millions of words said and unsaid, a lifetime born from nothing and extinguished in that same breath. The life we might have spent together. I had a passing thought of hope. But at the end of my exhale I shook my head and said, I don't know. Then I went back to my family and she went back to hers.

None of us said nothing the whole drive home from getting Darius out.

My moms at the wheel, eyes locked on the road ahead, Tekelle in the front passenger seat sneaking quick looks at me and Darius in the back. Darius just sat there, detached, slouched to the side with his forehead against the window, his eyes placing him somewhere else entirely. I could smell the blood that had dried on him. Sort of turned into an odor after a while, something that would stick on our clothes long after we had stripped them off.

When we pulled up to the curb in front of our house and our moms shut the car off, Tekelle asked her for the keys. She didn't say a thing, just dropped the keys in Tekelle's open palm and reached for her wallet on the dashboard. Tekelle held on to my arm while our moms and Darius stepped out and started walking to the front door. You make sure she don't kill him, Tekelle said. I'll go make sure Hera's alright. I nodded, kissed her on her cheek and left the car.

Mr. Johnson was outside, leaning on the chain-link fence that separated our home from his, watching Darius and my moms as they walked past.

You keep your head up, Elise.

My moms stopped and looked at him while Darius kept lumbering forward.

He still here, so it won't hurt forever, he said. Trust me on that.

She nodded gratefully and kept walking. He went and sat on his front steps. Right then, I wondered what it felt like to lose. He'd lost his only son a few years ago, his wife a few decades back. It changed him, took a toll on him. For a while I didn't think he was ever going to come outside again. But nowadays he always brought himself out to watch the kids play or listen to the neighborhood chatter or watch the cars pass. Nowadays, he looked like he was going to be okay.

But we weren't. The whole place had been blitzed. Everything that made our slender little townhouse a home, scattered and misplaced like gravity had taken a power nap: the collection of fridge magnets that held up our pictures, our pictures, the kitchen knick-knacks that had puns scrawled on them, the seasonings in the top cabinet above the stove that made the whole house smell good every Sunday dinner, the brass-framed portraits of family we'd never met that adorned our walls, all those invisible things we never thought about until they were out of place.

My moms ignored all that though. She paced while Darius sat on the couch, glanced out the window, paced again. Then she turned to him.

Now, she said mournfully, like she'd already braced to see one of her sons dead on the grass, let me tell you about dealing with the police.

Now let me tell you, that power of hers wasn't in what she did say, but what she didn't. She didn't say this was one of those milestone talks we all had to have, a coming-of-age on the sad way the world works, how we got here, where the parts had to go, all that. She didn't say this was one of those teachable moments, that everyone in life has loose ends, strands that keep us all together, and if fate has it tied that way, one end can bring about another. Everything she didn't say was in the tears that spilled gently from her eyes, in the quiver of her lips when the words just wouldn't come: Baby, I'm not mad at you, I'm mad at this world. But we don't have no choice but to live in it. Let's have a sit-down, just a talk. You not in trouble. It ain't nothing serious—just birds and bees.

Finishing the Harvest

Daniel Lassell

Preened for distribution with blade and rumble,
bales are hoisted up to the hay wagon,
organized thud-by-thud into a stack seven blocks high.
I have piled them into a barn and spaced them
foot-wide, so Kentucky doesn't swelter the loft into flame.
Though, maybe emptiness is too speedy a process.
And maybe oak branches, unable to touch the earth,
do envy these stems freed from their soil, split apart
and swimming into stomachs as livestock, animals, wind
will churn the finished harvest into one of their own.
Even pain can have an outward-traveling happiness,
a happiness like the kind you will find
in the passenger pickup lane at airports,
how people throw their jubilance out,
tossing it around bodies, saying "Hello" or "Welcome."
Watch the luggage straps, how they lift and place
with such an ease. Something you can let go,
when ready, from your fingers like joy.

LEARNING TO RATION

ANNELISE HATJAKES

Ada slips her hand into her pocket and thumbs her last remaining ration for joy. The intricately folded paper has worn thin from her rubbing it between her fingers like a rabbit's foot. But she doesn't do this for good luck. Her fingers are drawn to the torn stamp from her monthly ration book by a deep necessity—something animal and desperate—to know that it'll be there when she really needs it. The same used to be true for the two Xanax tablets hidden in a brown-orange prescription bottle she'd gingerly removed the label from. The bottle lay at the bottom of a plastic storage container labeled "Hair Stuff/Miscellaneous" under her bathroom sink. If the middle-of-the-night dry mouth and mile-a-minute thoughts hit her, she could easily unearth the bottle buried under cans of hairspray and cotton swabs and nail clippers. Knowing they were there was enough.

She stands in a line mostly composed of men, many with their hands in pockets too, and they're mumbling things profane in tone, but innocent in content. Their anger is kept on a leash like a dog they can't teach to heel. They probably can't wait to open up their crisp new books to the rage ration, tear it from the weak paper binding, and scream at anyone who happens to cross their paths. If she wanted to, Ada could sell those rations on the black market; she hasn't wanted to use one for God knows how long. Maybe it's the legally mandated mindfulness exercises she's been doing every other day.

The line is too long, and the grumbles around her are starting to merge and bend around her so that she feels like she's hearing them in surround sound at a movie theater where people have chosen seats too close to her own. She reaches into her pocket and rubs the paper, this time more gently.

As soon as she walks through her front door and sees her boyfriend's car key and bottle opener keychain, a darkly funny pairing when she thinks of his last two DUIs, she knows that he's there with another woman. She's known there was another woman for a long time. Has known it for so long, in fact, that she doesn't bother interrupting what's happening on the expensive memory foam mattress that she's still paying off in monthly installments. Instead, she waits until they're finished, then opens and closes the door louder than she did the first time. She hears them scramble for their clothes to a soundtrack of muffled panic, then hears a yelp and deduces that her boyfriend has stubbed his toe on the bed frame's leg. Ada begins to smile, but then reaches for her ration and forces her lips back into a neutral position. Now's not the time to use it.

She knows that she should feel hurt, consumed by a sense of loss now that this important part of her life's equation is being removed, but she doesn't. This is a natural, almost satisfying occurrence. It feels like watching raindrops on a window coalesce into a single stream that takes a predictable path down the pane, each droplet of expectation aligning with an outcome she saw coming.

Ada sits down on a bench at Ward Park, wedges headphones into her ears, and listens to her guided meditation playlist. The soothing voice instructs her to close her eyes and allow her body to be still. Feel the sensations in her body and be fully present with those sensations. Focus on her breathing. If her mind begins to wander, that's okay. Without judgment, simply return to the awareness of her breathing.

She pauses the playlist when a man limps over to her and says that he is very hungry and asks her if she can spare a dollar. He'll work for it, he promises. She wants to look in her wallet, but her rations for pity are all gone. These days, it seems like those always run out first. Ada wonders if her boyfriend used his when he got dressed and saw the post-it on the fridge that said "Love you to the moon" in her swirly script. Did it hit him when he recalled that she was forty-one and wasn't able to have a baby named Rosalie after her grandmother like she'd always wanted and her father had just died and her brother was still at Nevada Hopes Psychiatric Hospital, probably would never leave? Ada shakes her head at the man, then returns to the guided meditation.

Once again, she is focused on her breathing. But she thinks of her brother's gauze-wrapped wrists, the same wrists she used to wrap her hands around when she'd help him get out of the public pool. Without judgement, she tries to return to her breathing. But between the exhale and the inhale, she thinks of the woman who was just lying on her expensive mattress and her beautiful coworker's baby shower on Saturday and the raw patches of skin from her inner thighs chafing.

She cannot focus on her breathing. She opens her eyes and focuses instead on a marmot standing up on its hind legs, hands resting atop its fat belly. His lips are downturned, and she feels like if she got close enough and listened carefully enough, he may tell her a secret. She wonders what kinds of secrets a fat-bellied marmot has. He runs away as if he knows that she's onto him, and she laughs.

On her walk home, the sun makes her sweat, which brings a sting to her raw thighs. So, she tries to keep her strides short and her gate wide. She thinks of when she played hopscotch as a girl and felt the cool whoosh of air come under her skirt when her dress floated outward on each hop.

The thought cools her.

She thinks of the convertible their neighbor bought and let her ride in, with the top down even though it was forty degrees out.

The thought cools her. This time, even a shiver.

As she approaches her apartment, likely now empty, she reaches into her pocket, but all she feels are the thin layers of calloused skin that have formed on her fingertips.

Cuddlebug

Jenna-Marie Warnecke

8:44 am

Tuesday greets me with pale golden light, singing the song of the morning, the song of opportunity. I rise from my bed without using the snooze button even once, ready to meet the promise of the day, and I prepare my body and spirit for the world.

Before I step into the shower, I tap at the water to make sure it's not too hot. Hot water dries the skin, and as a man I take pride in keeping mine supple; not many cis males do. I luxuriate in a peppermint lavender blanket of antibacterial suds, speaking aloud an intention for the light scent to linger on my skin and instantly comfort this morning's first client. A matching body oil will help set the scent and soften the skin. I pay meticulous attention to the crevices other people neglect (behind the ears, between the toes, the fold of skin where leg becomes groin) and clean under my nails. I shave the stubble from my face as close as I can get it, but leave my chest hair alone—some people like chest hair—and apply leave-in conditioner to the hair on my head so it's ready for any fingers that may want to dive into it. I learned from my colleague, Nissa, that it's important to smell good, but not too strongly; you want to cleanse your client's nasal palate, not create new memories, lest they get too attached.

I stand naked before the full-length mirror and gaze at myself, work-ing my way into acceptance. I clear my throat and recite my mantra, pushing the words out from the center of my soul: "Manhood is a construct. Love is a practice. Practice love today."

I pack my Cuddle Bag, a duffel specially designed by Marc, the founder of the company, and decorated with round, genderless faces that smile or close their eyes in happy arches, and I head for the subway. As the M train crosses over the East River, Manhattan glittering with fresh daylight, I resist the urge to check the news on my phone. Evenings, when I can let go and cry and fret, are for the news; for now, I need to keep myself neutral and light. Instead, I check my Cuddlebug app for client info. Mrs. Norman, 84, UWS. Husband recently deceased. The poor dear. I'll have to give her some extra TLC today.

I can smell the mothballs and hear Mrs. Norman's television all the way from the elevator down the hall as I approach. At her door, I pull my shoulders back, smooth my hair and conjure a relaxed smile as I knock. A tiny, frail woman, dressed in a housecoat bursting with large purple pansies, opens the door, her wrinkled hand clutching the knob.

"Good morning, Mrs. Norman," I say, instantly inhabiting the persona of a beloved grandson or nephew. "My name's Michael, and I'll be your Cuddlebug today."

10:00 am

"Please, call me Maggie," Mrs. Norman says as she lets me in, pulling the door open into a massive living room filled with antiques and knickknacks, posters from art exhibitions dating back to the seventies crowding the walls, a grandfather clock nestled between two large windows looking out to Seventy-Fourth Street. "Can I get you some tea?" Mrs. Norman's—Maggie's—voice has the fragile, girlish quality of so many of the older women I've worked with, and I wonder how long ago her husband died, how long they'd been together.

"No, thank you," I reply, caressing her arm to acclimate her to my touch. "But may I use your bathroom to get changed?"

She shows me to the end of the hall, the smell of old urine emanating from the cluttered bathroom. There's a plastic donut on the toilet that makes it easier for her to go, and I make a mental note to be cognizant of bad hips. Mounds of white hair are threaded around the bristles of her brush on the counter. I change into my uniform, which can only be described as the world's best pajamas. Also designed by Marc, it's like an adult onesie, cut out of marvelously soft modal and specially made to be germ-repellant. It's V-cut at the neck to free tufts of chest hair or a maternal swell of cleavage, depending on who's wearing it. It's breathable, light, yet a definite barrier against nudity and, therefore, all kinds of unwanted (and unpaid-for) hanky-panky. In the winter we wear chenille Snuggies instead.

I find Maggie in her bedroom, which is overrun by junk—piles of jewelry on the vanity, unorganized papers on the desk, and the wall covered in framed portraits from what looks like the nineteen thirties. She's already in bed, facing toward me under a loosely crocheted blanket. I crawl in beside her, my six-foot-two body dwarfing hers, and pull her into my arms. Maggie sighs. Sunlight pours through the window. I feel the bones of her shoulders, her back, through the thin cotton of the purple pansies, and puffs of her coarse white hair brush against my chin, and I hold her close but not too tight and rub her back and push all the love I have out of my heart and into my arms. I wrap her in my love. Maggie makes a small noise, like a woodland animal, and burrows into me, and I know I'll get a good tip today.

I learned more about my colleagues' emotional health at New-Bug orientation than I had learned about my family in twenty-five years. Of course, there were a lot of folks with Mommy or Daddy issues; a handful of hippies hoping to save the world with affection, the physical manifestation of peace and harmony; there was even a former sex worker who just wanted a safer, gentler line of work. One woman, Patricia, said that living in the city had made her so aware of the loneliness of life on earth that she just couldn't take it anymore and decided to do something about it.

As for me, I have a micropenis. It's a certified medical condition. It's kind of just a fleshy nub, like a cocktail frank, on my lower pelvis, but it still works. In high school, my first (and last) girlfriend told me, "It's such a shame that a tall guy like you would have such a dinky thing." Apparently tall guys tend to have big penises. That's what I think when a girl flirts with me at a bar: she's just gonna be disappointed.

With Dawn—that was my girlfriend—I mastered all other forms of intimacy, but it wasn't enough. We only lasted a few months, and ever since then—through college and the first couple of years living here in the city— when I talk to a girl, I just can't wait for it to be over. *Please stop*, I want to say to her, *you're wasting your time*. I clam up, get all sweaty and weird, and eventually my wish comes true.

But I want to be better. I'm trying to be better. I went to a life-improvement seminar where the leader told us to say out loud, all at once, what we wanted more than anything. He counted to three and—as around me I heard cries of "happiness!" and "confidence!" and even one murmur of "a record contract"—I found myself shouting, "love!" My throat knotted up as soon as the word was out. The leader told us that the best way to get what you're lacking, be it respect or affection or kindness, is to give that same thing to the world, and you'll get it back one hundredfold. I'm not sure how the guy who wants a record contract will accomplish that, but mine seemed doable.

So I started doing public hugging before or after my shifts at Uniqlo. You know those people in Union Square Park who hold signs that say "Free Hugs"? That was me, and it was super empowering to be the one creating the love around me. I only got beat up once, pickpocketed twice. One day a woman came up to me and chirped, "I want a hug!" in that kind of tone that's both a shrug and an exclamation. She wasn't what you'd think of as heteronormatively "pretty," but there was something undoubtedly attractive about her. I folded my whole self around the woman's whole self, enveloping her in this truly full-bodied embrace, and something felt different. The hug took on an extra glow, a blazing energy like in a video game when you gain super power for a minute before going back to being Regular Mario. Hugging this woman, it was like two forces in the universe had finally locked together, and nothing could stop us; like the essence of existence itself was cycling between us in a figure eight of spiritual wholeness. Her body itself was the physical embodiment of a hug, both maternal and neutral, something you could lose yourself in, the human equivalent of a bouncy castle. That woman was Nissa.

I have no idea how long we were standing there like that. I have this Buddhist friend who says that a hug is not complete unless it's at least eight seconds long, and this experience just totally cemented that claim. When we pulled away, Nissa looked up at me and said, with an air of authority, "You're really good at that." When I found a Cuddlebug business card tucked into my pocket later that day, embossed on smooth linen paper stock with a phone number and a Midtown address, I knew exactly where it had come from. Nissa was a hugger like no other: she was a professional.

11:08 am

After my session with Maggie, during which she napped and farted a little, I accept a couple of bananas from her and go on my way. I've been trying to gain a little weight for maximum cuddleability, but it's super hard to do when you're vegan. You wouldn't believe how many avocado toasts I eat. But it seems to be working, as clients react to my body these days with less intimidation and more reciprocation.

Next on my list is Officer Reginald Pettigrew, 50, Woodside. I have a little time, so I go to the park and do a few sun salutations, then sit in the grass in a lotus position, meditating. A group of young French tourists take photos of me, but I don't mind. I silently wish them a great adventure and try my hardest to clear my heart of Mrs. Norman. This work requires a lot of emotional energy, and Nissa taught me that if you don't take a few minutes between clients to "reset," by the end of the day you'll be a mess. Once, during my first week, I just rushed from client to client with no break between, and that night I found myself weeping uncontrollably at an episode of "The Simpsons." Later I cried myself to sleep, the tears on my pillow holding the poison of all the sadness I'd absorbed throughout the day. As I finally drifted into slumber, it felt as though *I* were being held, comforted by an invisible force. Like the universe was cuddling *me*.

I try to be as mindful as possible of people's energies, both at and outside of my work. I've thought about becoming a physical therapist, but I'm not sure if it's hands-on enough. I trained for awhile to become a massage therapist, but I couldn't deal with the many different bodily fluids that accidentally came out of people all the time. It's also really hard on the hands, which cuddling isn't. Cuddling is less dangerous, more "daylight," than prostitution, though you do have to be very careful not to let a client become sexually aroused. This can be super difficult, because when a person who desperately craves touch is held in perfect, unconditional sweetness, there can be an overflow of emotion that is easily conflated with love, and of course love is always mixed up with sex, and occasionally things do get out of hand. There aren't a lot of guys who do this job, because they risk unwanted erections each time. Luckily, I don't have that problem. If I ever get accidentally turned on, it's very rare that anyone would notice.

I breathe in warm, late-summer air, and with each exhalation I give Mrs. Norman my love. Inhale scent of roasted nuts at a nearby vendor cart, exhale a pantheistic prayer for Mrs. Norman's peace and happiness. Inhale the smell of a dog evacuating its bowels a few feet away, and, finally, a last exhalation, releasing Mrs. Norman from my life. *I am not responsible for her*, I remind myself. *I can only provide comfort for her journey.*

12:32 pm
Officer Pettigrew's house reminds me of the one my father lived in right after he and my mom got divorced: dark, lined in wood paneling, full of outdated furniture. I half-expect to see a poster of Kathy Ireland on the wall and a row of empty beer cans along the kitchen windowsill, but instead there's a single potted succulent, basking in the noon sun, and white-capped bottles of heart medication.

Officer Pettigrew is quite the opposite of Mrs. Norman: stout and gruff, shaped by a round belly and decorated in flaky skin. He has the standard-issue cop mustache. I shake his hand with both of my hands, giving his shoulder a little pat, which makes him jump. He shifts from foot to foot as I look at photos of his teenage sons in maple wood frames. "You, uh, want a beer or something?" he asks, scratching his scalp, then hands on hips.

"No, thank you so much," I reply, pushing warmth into my voice. In the bathroom I change into a second Cuddlesuit, the first in a Ziploc bag in the duffel, then place my hands over my heart and close my eyes. *He needs you*, I tell myself. *How can you improve his life? How can you redirect his energy?*

I meet Officer Pettigrew in the bedroom he shares with his wife. He's sitting on the edge of the bed, back straight, fidgeting.

"Big or little?" I ask.

"Huh?" he grunts, eyes flashing, chin jerked toward me.

"Would you rather be the big spoon or the little spoon?"

"Oh, uh … I dunno, I guess big." He laughs without pleasure. "Look, I'm not gay or nothing."

I shrug. "Me neither."

"To be honest, I've never done this before."

"I understand," I say. "The good news is, there's no wrong way to cuddle. You just relax, and I'll handle everything."

I instruct him to close his eyes. I take one of his hands and massage it in fast, hard rubs that move up and down the forearm to get him comfortable with contact, then do the other hand. "The first thing I want you to know is that you're not alone," I tell him, rubbing my hands up and down his shoulders like a coach giving a pep talk. "We're a very successful business for a reason. And the second thing I want you to know is that this world is better because you're in it." Officer Pettigrew looks up at me with eyes that glisten with something like fear. Fear that I'd seen him, who he really is, maybe.

I slide into the bed and Pettigrew climbs in behind me, stiffly placing his short arms over mine. I nuzzle up to him, fitting the pieces together, and he rests his cheek on my back. Outside, children ride their bikes and scream in delight.

"How long have you lived in this neighborhood?" I ask, trying to help him relax.

"Almost twenty years."

"That's nice. And you have children?"

"Yeah, two sons." I feel his breath is shallow, his arms rigid, and I know he's having trouble letting go. He must have seen so much in his life, and it's all stuck inside of him. Imagine carrying that around with you all the time. He must be exhausted.

"Do you ever wonder which one of them will die first?" I ask. It seems cruel, but sometimes the release valve needs to be turned. I want him to get his money's worth, after all.

Pettigrew is silent, then I feel his body begin to shake behind me. He clings so hard to me that I reach up and caress his hand. "Breathe, Reggie," I whisper, and I hear his throat open, and Officer Pettigrew lets out a wet, jagged wail that sounds like it's been trapped in him for years.

"I think about it all the time," he sobs, hugging me tight. I hear the mucus of his sadness choking his throat, his nasal passages, until suddenly he releases me. "I changed my mind," he announces, pulling away. "I wanna be the little spoon." We roll over in tandem and I pull him close to me, hugging his round body, tight as a tire. *The love you give is only a fraction of what you'll receive.* I nestle my nose into his neck, rubbing his arm and soothing him with shushes just like my grandma used to do.

I've been trying to get my roommate, Dahlia, to be a cuddler. She's training to become an ayahuasquera but works a day job selling PowerBuch, a kombucha energy drink, with her boyfriend in Bushwick. She doesn't have the typical cuddler body—she's super willowy, with long, branchlike arms—but she has flowy blonde hair and ridiculously soft skin. She may be skinny, but Dahlia's energy is so beautiful, I just know she'd be a really successful Cuddlebug.

Nissa's the perfect Bug. She trained me. Nissa brings you into her arms and you can, like, literally feel love radiating from her body into yours, seeping into your skin like lotion. She laughs from the bottom of her stomach, the sound of it filling her whole chest and tumbling out of her, and when she laughs, even at the littlest thing, it feels like you're the greatest person on earth. She treats you like you're the bee's knees, and that's the secret to repeat business: making sure your client feels totally loved,   accepted, and cared for.

It's not a lie, either… or, at least, you try for it not to be. I've had some challenging situations—bodies large and small, some crippled, some severely lacking in hygiene or self-care—but you try to open your heart and see some-thing special and lovable in each person. The thing you have to keep in mind is, every single human *needs* love and affection. It's not just reserved for the kind and the beautiful. Fatsos and bums need it, angry Wall Street brokers need it, drugstore cashiers and bus drivers are desperate for it. A woman once hired me to cuddle her baby. Just to hold him. Poor thing was wracked with postpartum hormones and she was convinced that her holding of this baby wasn't full enough of love. "He can tell," she told me in a tight whisper, her cheeks sunken and sallow. "He knows I can't do it."

2:02 pm
Sierra, 25, lives in Greenpoint, in a gigantic loft with exposed brick and plants hanging from the ceiling. She answers the door in her bathrobe, young and beautiful with flushed cheeks, wavy brown hair, and catlike eyes. She has the kind of body I like for a girl, straight-backed with the thick, tight curves of someone who dances for a living. As I enter the apartment, my senses detect the whiff of fresh sex, that oddly moist, salty smell that's like a gelatinous beach. There's a muscular young man by the bed buttoning his shirt, and he furrows his brow when he sees me.

"Who the fuck is this?" he asks Sierra.

"He's my Cuddlebug."

"Cuddlebug?" The guy looks sideways at me. "Like those signs from the subway?"

"That's right. He's here to lay with me since you insist on leaving immediately after we fuck." Sierra inspects her nails.

"Are you serious?" the guy asks.

"You can get changed behind that partition," Sierra says to me, gesturing to a Japanese-style portable wall on the other side of the loft. I hear them arguing as I pull the third Cuddlesuit over my body, surrounded by flimsy bras and silk dresses. When I emerge, the guy looks at me and laughs. "That's fucked up," he says to Sierra.

"You're welcome to stay longer next time," she calls as he heads for the door. "Save me a couple bucks." The door slams and she sighs, then takes my hand and walks me to the bed. She faces me and we tumble in together, and our bodies instantly fit. We lace our legs around each other's as though we've done this a million times; she pushes her breasts into the flat part of my chest, scoots her pelvis into the negative space my hips create. I press my palms against her back; she releases a deep breath. "I met him on Tinder," she explains. "It's just impossible to get everything you want from one person anymore."

"I know, honey. I'm sorry," I say, rubbing her back and trying to play the part of gay BFF, though all I can think about as she complains about men and her dance company and her waitressing side gig is the feeling of her nipples through her robe. I feel them brush against mine even through the Cuddlesuit. I run my hands through Sierra's hair, enjoying its fruity scent, and listen to her whine about a fight she had with her best friend, who didn't heart her most recent Instagram post, and I think how l ovely it would be to wake up next to someone like her. How we could shop at the farmer's market and make love in the moonlight and hold the weight of each other's bodies in partner yoga. I've planned out our whole life together based on a single nipple.

"Mmm," Sierra purrs when she finally stops talking and tucks further into me. She kisses my neck, then my chin, and when I look down at her, she tries to kiss my lips but I put my hand over her mouth, as if to silence her. She kisses my palm instead.

"Are you sure?" she says. She takes my hand and guides it to the hot, muffled space between her legs. I close my eyes and clear my throat. I'm flooded with warmth and I feel my heart pound, the mark of the start of a dangerously selfish sensation. The feel of her is overwhelmingly pleasant, easy; I haven't experienced it in such a long while. I try to be present, to absorb every detail to replenish my memory of this kind of intimacy for all the nights that lay ahead. But I know I can't let her do this; I can't let myself do this. *It's not real*, I remind myself. *She's paying you.* But it's not so easy to throw away everything you want when it's quite literally in hand.

I force myself to meditate on the tall-guy rule, breathing into it until I'm strong enough to withdraw my hand. I place it in the valley between her shoulder blades and savor the softness of her legs entwined with mine. "I'm sure," I nod. "Just like you said...you can't get everything from one person."

3:30 pm

The Cuddlebug headquarters are in a nondescript office building in Midtown. It's where you come if you don't want or have time for a house call. We get a lot of people on their lunch hour or instead of a coffee break, popping in for a midday shot of compassion and kindness.

The space itself is open and sunlit with individual rooms called Cuddle Pods. On my way to the employees-only area, I pass a giant cuddle puddle in the center of the main room, where Nissa anchors a dozen or so people nestled against one another, stroking each other's arms, squeezing each other close on top of a pile of oversized pillows. Nissa's eyes light up when she sees me and she tosses me a genuine smile of ecstasy, closing her eyes and rocking a man in her bosom, her face a living emoticon.

"Thanks for coming in on such short notice," Marc says in the locker room, handing me a fresh Cuddlesuit. "There was a shooting at a mall this morning, and with another neo-Nazi rally last week and the attacks in Europe ... well, we've just been slammed." Marc doesn't look like your typical Bug— he wears a tailored suit every day and slicks his hair back, his face constantly pinched near a grimace. I suspect he started Cuddlebugs in order to be its first (and best) customer.

"I understand," I say, taking the suit from him and tossing the used ones into a laundry basket.

"So, today, we're going for comforting, protective, super-reassuring," says Marc, gesturing with practiced hands like he's at a sales pitch. "You're Daddy, you're the ultimate boyfriend, you're Keanu Reeves in *Speed*."

"Got it," I nod. "I'm just going to shower, and then should I join Nissa in the cuddle puddle?"

"No, I need you in one-on-ones for now," Marc frowns. "We want people to be feeling comforted by young men today, to balance the fear of them."

I spend the rest of my afternoon in an ultra-soft bed in a soundproof room lit by lavender candles, holding one person after another: a middle-aged woman whose children in college don't call her; an advertising executive who lost a big client this morning; a Virginia Tech alum. One young woman breathes solely in sighs as she ticks off her list of fears: nuclear bombs, dirty bombs, regular bombs... Some people are quiet and just want to be held; some talk my ear off, and just want to be heard. I hold them all and tell them I'm there for them, and I mean it. I make myself mean it.

At the end of each session we give our clients iced mint tea and sit with them until they're ready to leave. We don't rush anybody. If I see any of them on the street, I'll act like we've never met. The people who call on us do it mostly out of shame, the embarrassment of needing love, needing to be touched. Maybe one day I'll get tired of it, of selling my affection. But for now, I need it too. Like everybody else, I'm still learning how to be okay. Sometimes, like when I'm entangled with a beautiful girl like Sierra, or wrapped in the arms of a man older and taller than me, and I smell his Old Spice cologne and hear his heart beating, slow and steady against my cheek, I'm filled up with inner light and for once I feel glad, and good, and grateful. In those moments, I think maybe my clients should be the ones charging me.

But today doesn't have that aura. My final client of the day used to be a soldier in Afghanistan, and he doesn't say a word. He just lies in my arms and clutches my back and soaks my Cuddlesuit in tears. I try to give him everything that's left in me. "Do you feel better?" I ask him, rubbing his shoulders, as he rises at the end of our session. The man shrugs, head bowed, and slips out the door without ever once having met my eyes.

6:13 pm

When I'm done for the day, I sit in my Cuddle Pod, palms pointed to the heavens, and try to release everyone from my heart. I count every single one of them like petals off a flower and imagine myself tossing the petals onto the wind, watching them float away in a silky confetti of varied colors. I spend twenty minutes doing this, but it doesn't feel like enough. My head is throbbing and my chest feels hollow. My energy is, like, the opposite of blocked: I feel like I've consumed too much and given too much and my love is unharnessed and spilling out from every pore. I just want to go home and curl up in the arms of someone who wants me, someone like Sierra. I look at her picture on the app—she gave me five stars—and I wonder, just for like *half* a second, whether I should go back to her loft and call her bluff. But the risk— of her rejecting me, laughing at me, or worse, hiding her disgust behind a polite, pitying smile—or, heck, the risk of me inadvertently starting the next #MeToo wave with inappropriate Cuddlebug behavior—is just too great. I decide to go home, and if Dahlia is there, I'll ask her to cuddle me instead.

I leave the CBHQ and walk toward Bryant Park, avoiding the people who amble down the middle of the sidewalk staring at their phones, everyone connected and alone, and I smoke an American Spirit cigarette I bummed from a woman in a skirt suit on the street. I know it's super bad for me, but sometimes it's the only thing that makes me feel better. It's a leftover habit from my angry teenage years, and a nice little rebellion, because I could *never* smoke before cuddling a client. I only smoke at the end of the day, when I know no one else will be in my arms.

For a long time, I felt sorry for myself because of my body; of course,

I got bullied in school and couldn't experience relationships the way my peers could. I thought I would never experience the kind of passion I saw in the movies or on TV. Rap videos where women clung to a man two or three at a time made me burn with envy. But being a Cuddlebug has changed that. I remind myself of this fact as I exhale smoke near the entrance to the subway, taking my time to finish the cigarette. With my job, I get to meet other people who are lacking in love, and that makes me feel good; it helps me to not feel alone, seeing others being lonely. I see that not everyone gets what they need, and that it's okay to need anyway. I see that a romantic relationship is not the only way to give or receive love. *I give it, and get it, all day every day*, I tell myself, and not one of those people measures my value by the size or shape of my penis. So I don't either. It's enough just to feel I have a purpose in life, something I'm good at.

I begin my journey back to Brooklyn. On the platform at 42nd Street I see an older man doing magic tricks for a dollar, and I feel his aching, his longing for contact. I give him a twenty, which is not as good. Little things like that, especially on a day like today, can make me gush with sadness—an old person walking slowly across the street, a person with a shaking, palsy hand. A frustrated parent, or a homeless person folded over themselves on the sidewalk will do it to me. New York should come with a trigger warning. *May not be suitable for some viewers*, you know? Something as simple as a woman wearing outdated makeup or an ill-fitting pair of jeans is enough to incite a cascade of empathy in my chest. It's a real, physical feeling. It's thick and black, inky, and sticks to my bones until I do something good for someone. Dahlia says I try too hard to heal the world; she calls me Atlas. Then she puts her hand on my chest and says I have to heal that first. This is the conversation we have every time we're stoned.

That dark, sticky feeling wells up in me as I board the M train heading downtown. I can't stop thinking of the soldier, the quiet choke of his sobs muffled against my chest. I can't shake the feeling that I failed him. I did a lot of good work today, but somehow I feel so heavy, you could squeeze me out like a sponge. I should have taken more breaks this afternoon. It's rush hour and all around me, people hold their bodies tight, arms crossed over their chests, making themselves as compact as possible or scooting away from their neighbor to avoid touching each other. In this city you can be lonely but never alone, and New Yorkers have amazing ways of creating their own intimate spaces, even in a crowd.

You can see incredible things about people when they don't know you're watching them, as on the train: every age they've been—the business-man who folds his hands in his lap and reads an ad above the seat across from him, eyes wide, looking like a child—and their worst selves, the glaring side eyes, the jabs, the tight lips. One woman shoots another one a dirty look when the second lady's bag bumps up against her shoulder. She looks enraged, and over what? I think of a story I read last week of a disturbed man who shoved a woman in front of an oncoming train, just because she'd brushed past him in her hurry down the stairs.

A wave of sorrow washes over me, so I close my eyes and cherish the feeling of other people's bodies against mine. *I'll take it*, I tell them telepathically. *I will absorb the touches you shy away from. We are all one.* I make myself hyperaware of the soft, sweaty sides and sharp elbows of all the lonely people around me, grateful for every second and every inch of flesh against my flesh, hoping to spread my positive vibrations out to them like a heat lamp. I try to pick out as many scents as I can: all the different strains of B.O., sour and bitter and salty; the floral perfumes and powdery deodorant scents mingling. *Your air is cuddling; why can't you be okay with each other?* I think as the lady next to me sighs and shoves me, more people cramming in at Fourteenth Street.

I open my eyes, and before me is a brawny man who keeps clenching and releasing his fist. He looks like my father. His lips are pressed together, face red, beads of sweat gathering at his hairline, and he is the most in need of a hug of anybody I've seen in a long, long time. He must feel so bad inside. I feel tears swelling in my eyes, my throat tight, and I reach up and rub his shoulder to assure him that everything's going to be okay.

He jumps and swats my hand away. "What the fuck are you doing?" he shouts.

I know I'm not supposed to approach strangers in this way; usually I would just slip my card in his pocket and wait for him to come to me. They always do. But today, I can't help it. Deep in my heart, my intuition is screaming that this man needs me, now. I have so much to give, and he is so empty, and maybe if I correct the imbalance between us, the whole world will be somehow, in some way, just a little more at peace. And we need every shred of it that we can get. "You are loved," I tell him, tears spilling out of me, trying to pierce his soul with my kind eyes. *And what about me?* my heart wants to know. I reach out to him again, hoping to tenderly stroke his cheek.

"Don't touch me, you fucking faggot," he snarls with a hard shove, sending me in a trust fall into a handful of people, all of us losing our balance together as the train rocks. It truly feels as though the group of us has become one collective being.

"Who do you think you are, huh, you little punk?" The man spits on me. Everyone's staring as my brethren pull themselves up and the doors open at West Fourth Street. Folks pour out and flood in as I struggle to get upright, trying to disembark and wait for the next M train, but I fall at the threshold, skinning my palms. As I crawl out, an overweight teenage girl trips on me in her rush to get in before the doors close, and I strive not to let her fall, and my Converse sneaker gets stuck in the gap between the train and the platform, and everyone is just walking right past me as I shout to the conductor.

"Wait!" I try so hard to make my voice heard, but my throat is so knotted up with sadness and panic that it comes out a squeak. The conductor's head is turned the other way. I bang on the silver door, but the people inside the train look into the distance, music in their ears, or read their phones.

I manage to pull myself free just in time, and I hug my knees to my chest as the M departs the station. The wind of the receding train blows my tears to the back of my cheekbones. I hold myself tight. The rest of New York walks around me, hurrying to make their connections, on their way home to whoever.

Self-Portait as an Apostle of Longing

Sara Henning

I.
What one calls hijinks, another calls gospel,
       like Hemingway jotting six words on a napkin—
          For sale: baby shoes. Never worn. This is how novels
          are born. A real fool's miracle. I believe in whimsy,
     the uncanny cells that bind us. Blood jets rendering
a story smooth. *Mother died too young. Miss her.*

Are you still reading? *Still missing her. No more words.*
       Imagine this heroine, black down to her underwear.
          She's a Mothra incognito, a bad mama jama
          cresting through every deus ex machina like another
     stage of grief. Tell me you'd watch her dark night
of the soul, breathless as she breaches her cocoon.

          Hard as jade, you could love her. Right? You could
pity her story until a genre explodes.

II.

Pity her story until a genre explodes—when my mother
      said *Love is how you suffer together*, I heard *Marry the nice boy,*
            not the boy you'd rather fuck. I heard, love is the bruise

         a boy always leaves, thumbprints like ghosts of blackberries.
     I didn't marry the nice boy, Mother. I'm still breathing
in the love you always feared, how sudden it is,

how ugly it can be when it unsutures its hold—
      yellow-green love like the moon in heat. Crescent, waxing,
         half illumined gibbous love, or the moon-is-always-turning-
vascular kind of love. In other words, love undoing itself,
     seeking a center. Forgive me, Mother, when I mean to say—
love forms my body's reckless galaxy. Make of me

      love's naturalized citizen, when I mean to say,
when I mean to say—*My body: where do I end?*

III.

My body: where do I end? I'm five, and she's cutting sharp
      into a Winn Dixie parking lot, our car sideswiped by a Sedan.
         Her torso struck with the airbag's punch, then glass splintering.

      Glass in my face. A whole history fractured in that moment
     hanging, limboed by heat, another spring glitzing
through fissure, the lilt of car exhaust—I said—*My body:*

where do I end? How long until her voice is a hush
      I can't refuse? I used to map the scars on her hands—
         glass from the windshield like a fractal

      bisecting her palms. Hot oil feathering
     her thumb's lush pith. She called it a Luna moth,
the scar eclipsing her thumb and index finger, the pulsing spot.

      Evidence we can be erased. As if to say, love
is a wound that feels like longing. *It traps us. It consoles us.*

IV.

It traps us. It consoles us—her IV drip of morphine,
       the Stanley Cup playoffs blazing on the TV
            nurse Linda rigs toward her hospice bed.

           The Penguins lead the Sharks, but coma filches her away
       before the win: 4-2. Liver necrosis drops its gloves,
then hoists her past the final scrimmage. My mother: a trophy

refracting a light already gone. I'm not saying love is a circle
       that will not end. I'm not saying love is only the wound
            that won't close. I'm only saying love

           is the way we finally say yes to the world.
      Not her oxygen tank littering the La-Z-Boy. Not her battle
to breathe. I want love as strong as her cellular chain. If love

           must break us to make us holy, then tell me, Mother—
is it the world or your blood still clenching me?

V.

Is it the world or your blood still clenching? If love must break us
       to make us holy, then grief is my church. My mother
           taught me to hide the Host of loneliness inside me, another

           perjure of faith between my teeth. To repeat these words,
      these grievances intersecting—*Holy, holy.* I'm tearing Sunbeam
bread for the gulls in my dreams now, salt and crushed shell

glazing my paradise lost. Those years, I watched her
       in a strapless one-piece turn golden under a hymn of oil.
           She'd rub aloe where the skin peeled off, blisters marking

           a glitz-born violence in her skin. Planets made shapeless
      by plasma unhusk her epithelial heat, then freckle.
How can all of this unfurl now in a cloisonné urn?

           Still, I envy the ghost-gulls, their run-float after every sliver.
Pilgrims of ether, I long for their salt-bleached faces.

VI.

It's true: I'm a pilgrim of ether. I'm an apostle of longing.
    While getting married, yellow's nude haint had
            a rendezvous with my bridal lace. I spoke my vows,

            yellow slinking up on me like a clade of wasps.
    You could hear its blatant murmur against my throat,
its risk getting handsy with the small of my back. Every fleur de lis

within reach was graffitied by our lady of the torrent: Yellow,
    yellow everywhere. A deliberate, piss-bright heat.
            It means one thing, my husband whispered: *your mother's with us,*

            and her ghost is raising hell. Pity my rhinestone tiara,
    my glass of prosecco. Even the cake was spiked—
nothing survived her blaze. For an RSVP,

            my mother preached her gripes. In every picture,
I'm a flash of torched vanilla. I downright radiate.

VII.

If I could hawk you a line so smooth it radiates,
    I'd quote the Gospel of Grief. I'd deliver a sermon:
            six words can preach, bear witness. Their pith can testify!

            I'd doctor you sequels with names like *A story after the world ended*
    or *Lovely Apocalypse: a whole new normal*, until their Hail
Marys vibrate your blood: *Things are okay.*

Every lost daughter would abandon her loop of shame—
    Mother, forgive me—and mercy herself. How can I woo you
            with my true grief song, "One Winter Tuesday, an MRI"?

            An eight-pound tumor rambling through my mother's colon
    is eager to jazz up her uterine walls all night. *A sick*
bass shred will trigger. A highway man, he's two-stepping his way

            to her womb. *A rock-anthem refrain will blossom through*
her throat: rogue angel, don't take my breath before you go.

VIII.

Oh mother of the last breath, oh mother of the failed liver,
    oh mother of the tumor fruiting in the dark.
        Begin again. *Oh mother of wild persimmons*

        in her liver ducts, oh mother of harvest starring her lungs.
    Again. *Oh mother of the last bowel movement*
less shit than blood, oh mother of the BiPAP mask,

oh mother of the living room hospital bed,
    oh mother of the coma. As if to say—*oh mother*
        of the last meal, oh mother who no longer

        drinks water, she's so busy drinking the last of God
    from the air. It happens this way, the body a color
radiating shamelessly: *love tongue, mother tongue,*

        as if to say— *I'm a slipshod puddle of light.*
Or, between tongue and glottal stop—*holy.*

IX.

Dear Mother, I'm ashamed. I've forgotten what's holy.

    The past is hijinks, not blood jets. Grief wore me smooth.
    People say we look alike when a picture snaps me

        with my head thrown back, my laugh all horse teeth and sass.
    And sometimes, a pull off of an unfiltered cigarette
and you're here like hard jade, another dark night of the soul.

Sometimes, I dream of your steel-blue eyes, wake up
    with them instead of my own. Which is to say, *God*
        is the geometry guiding our mercy. I want to say love

        is the cigarette smoke haunting a heaven without you in fewer words.
    To win a bet like Hemingway. To pity a genre
that's never been mine. So I say—*The dusky half-life*

        is most familiar. Do you believe me? Can you forgive me?
So I say—*That dangerous intimacy, throaty and beautified.*

The Web

Bill Capossere

I first noticed the web strung between the garage wall and the top step just outside our door last week when, transferring a spider from our kitchen sink to the outdoors, I unwittingly dropped her directly onto its strands, making her a victim of my obliviousness to what lay just outside my door.

And if this were another essay, I might track this thread of thought across a whole host of examples of said obliviousness—the myriad of ways in which we move through this world blind to what lies all around us, below our feet and above our heads, and how over time I've tried to teach myself to see just a little more, to pull back the fabric our hurried lives hang between us and not-us, to catch a moment's longer glimpse of what lies in the unlit corners.

If this were that essay, I'd have to rope my nine-year-old son—my most important tutor in this endeavor—into the action. But then he'd bring with him his magnifying glasses; his collection bottles; two insect nets—one for delicate captures, one for beating the brush with; pinning boxes; vials of pond water in various shades of inky green (which bring themselves a host of items: stentors and rotifers and euglena, daphnia and cyclops and, if he's lucky, tentacled hydra); craft organizers filled with dead insects, feathers, pine cones, seeds, and leaves; his habitats—homes for mail-order specimens and science-class refugees and general "Can we take that home?" creatures: giant millipedes, salamanders, darkling beetles, praying mantises, harvester ants, Giant Madagascar Hissing Cockroaches, and assorted spontaneous discoveries from around the house, the yard, and the hiking trails; his microscope—superior to the one I used in either my tenth grade biology class or my freshman biology class at Syracuse; all those rocks (don't get me started on all those rocks); that strange piece of something we have no idea what it is but it must be worth paying attention to because we prized it out of the soil or the bark or the moss or from under the fridge and kept it; that other strange piece of something we have no idea what it is; his meandering, time-disdaining gait; and his eyes—those gloriously wide-to-the-unveiled-world eyes.

I usually leave spiders wherever I come across them in the house, content to cede them their out-of-the-way corner domicile or step over their floorboard hunting ground, but this one had no home, having hitched a ride on one of our garden vegetables before scampering out from the peppers, beans, and okra piled in the sink, trying to avoid the draining swirl of brown water. I lay my hand down in her path, let her crawl atop my index finger, and then, because my wife was watching even as she pretended not to, opted to transport her outside rather than just drop her on the counter as I normally would have done to watch her meander under the microwave or behind the fruit basket, ready to herd her away from the stove, the still-hot tea kettle, the sink I'd just pulled her from.

And if I *were* constructing a different essay—different from this one or the previously mentioned alternative—or if I had a different wife, this would be where I might talk about all those potentially troublesome moments of decision-making in a relationship that you thought you'd both foreseen and aired out before the marriage: children or no children, religion or no religion, this school district or that school district, joint or separate accounts, good paying burdensome jobs or low-paying happier employment, meat or no meat; except it would not be these but all those other unforeseen choices that turned out to be more telling: paper or plastic, shampoo bottle on the shelf at the front of the shower or on the back corner of the tub, beer bottles in front of the huge container of juice in the fridge or behind it, bookstores or libraries, Macs or PCs, killing spiders or leaving them. All of them leading to the essay in which I mine as a writer the tiniest of moments that have forced we two to face some starkly unpleasant truths about the other.

Except we don't have many of those moments, my wife and I. Almost none at all, in fact. Turns out that what all those unexpectedly revelatory moments reveal is just how well suited we are for each other (or at least how tolerant my wife is). Unless what we hide from each other is too darkly sly to be lured out by the mundane actions of our everyday lives, scuttling about in the subterranean warrens of our personal worlds, or lying still and hidden in the darkened corners, muttering silky congratulations to itself on staying secreted.

Where it will have to stay, since this is not that essay.

So, under my wife's watchful eyes, I walked over to our side door, opened the screen, and held out my arm, waiting patiently while the spider slowly unspooled her way downward.

At a point just about level with our top step though, she suddenly stopped descending, hanging there still a few feet from the ground. When I directed my gaze past her hovering body, I realized I'd suspended her over a large web whose one edge was anchored to the side of the step. I raised my hand to lift her up, but either she was already held fast or my movement was too abrupt, because the slender thread connecting us simply parted, no sense of pressure or force, just the thin evidence of a silky white line eddying in unfelt currents of air a few inches below my finger.

And here you can probably see yourself where this might spin right into a meditation on the fragility of what binds us, all of us, one to the other. You've got the visuals—the two of us at each end of the spider's silk, then the severed thread waving in the breeze. You can see where it all might go.

And if I gather around my hands like skeins of yarn all the frayed threads of my life, respool them toward me and examine each end for telltale signs, what remnants will I find of the former lives once tethered to the other side? This one led to my Aunt's easy cackle, here to my   Grandmother's weighty arms kneading dough or stirring sauce or crocheting, this to my Grandfather's head—round and bobbing and red amid the tomatoes, here to my Uncle Tom—though I hesitate to pull it; he was always the trickster.

My father's stocky smile was at the end of this one, along with the low rumble of the garage door rising shortly after five o'clock through the family room walls, the smell of tobacco and T-shirt beside me as I pedal a newly bought bike. Over here lay the crackle of my mother's hair beneath the bristles as I brushed it newly grown out, as well as how she sang Christmas carols—badly but loudly, a trait I've inherited—and how big she looked from the kitchen floor when I looked up from my Legos and dinosaurs, when five feet of linoleum seemed all the wide expanse of the world that would ever come between us, nothing so large that it couldn't be bridged by a throw of rope or a spinneret's thread.

Feeling now a little bad about the turn of events, and also a bit curious if my spider would be able to trace an escape from a web not of her own making, I kneeled down for a closer look.

Her first movements were cautious—shy, tentative touches, trying to avoid perhaps the thrumming signal which would call out her waiting kind. Despite the soft movement, though, first one leg, then another slowly became stuck, and as I watched her struggle to free herself, the pale rounded body pulsing up and down along the thread, I began to feel a growing sense of guilt. I had, after all, carried her outside so as to avoid drowning her and while I could appreciate the several ironies at play, the whole situation seemed a bit unjust. So, trying to destroy as little of the web as possible, I rescued her a second time, curling my two fingers under her and gently tearing away a tiny acre of silk, then walking over to the lawn before letting her wind her way free from my cupped hands and into the concealing green slivers of grass.

And were this yet a fourth kind of essay, I might weave in my son again on a sailing string of metaphor. Because isn't this just what I will eventually have to do with this child I pluck again and again from sticky situations—from bee stings and bullies, from too-fragile branches and rock-climbing walls that turn out to be higher than they first appeared, from nine-year-old girls who won't leave him alone and nine-year-old girls that do—uncup my hands and release him out into a world whose sharp edges can slice as easily as that knife locked away in the childproofed drawer? A world where danger is not contained to the top shelf or confined beyond the gated stairs, whose blows are not cushioned by bumpers or foam, and whose shadowed recesses will hide not only unseen risks but cloak his very path away from me so that soon he will be a retreating figure, a wave of undulating grass, a still silence, then a memory of noisy peril and need, then not even that for me.

I've been watching the web outside our door ever since then, tracking its steady geometric progress. Each afternoon, before entering our house, I kneel down on the stairs and measure with my eyes the web's woven advance. It took two days for the breach I had made to be repaired, and in the week since, the web as a whole has expanded two or three inches, so that in the middle of its curved edge it extends beyond the step itself.

When I leave for school in the early morning, the dew glitters along its lines, a silver-stranded net from stair to wall, waterdrops like stars, and as my foot drops onto each step the entire web sways slightly from the sudden tremor, a shudder of tiny constellations. Multiplied a hundred times through the multifaceted lenses of a spider's eye, it must appear, I think, the very end and beginning of time.

Which is this essay. And, it turns out, all those others as well.

THE GIRL WHO SURVIVED BY PRETENDING TO BE A CORPSE

ROY BENTLEY

Imagine how motionless she needed to be. And at once.
She said she copied Embassy statuary, aping tranquility

if not the dark insolence at the heart of everything male.
Said that the soldier-shapes kicked dirt over them. This,

after God stopped shielding her, declaring it was her job.
When it was quiet, she started pushing up with her legs,

steering herself over and through the arms of the fallen.
Who knew there was this italicizing brightness to stars

that didn't so much penetrate the loose soil as imbue it.
That night, a young woman found in herself the resolve

to rise and be dusted off by a wallow for water buffalos.
To insist on a next and next breath, and call that *Justice*.

THE TROPIC

MATTHEW FITCH

Yþ am Eldric. Eldric is myn Goth name & *yþ* is myn personal pronoun. though yþ am other than Goth, yþ accept the label.

yþ am watching MTV æt Malthe's after school. *Malthe* is Malthe's real name from hwanne he was born across the sea in Danemark. Malthe is not Goth, though we agree that if he were, *Malthe* would be Goth enough.

he points his chin æt the blank screen:

here it comes—

crap, yþ think, but tis a moment later true: the first insistent *Yo*. the bright brass chord explodes: *there* is the stitching on the Yankees cap; *now* the bill flips up to show the knit furric eyebrows & the crossed rapping eyes looking out æt the world like a puzzled, mean-looking puppy. The Tropic retreats from the camera & the TV rattles his beat.

The Tropic raps about his hard times & his love life. yes, things have been hard, but hwanne the scene changes to a sunswept pile of rocks by the sea yþ know—once again—that he has overcome:

he spreads his arms wide; a wind flutters his long-tailed shirt clear from his waist & his pale abs contract for emphasis as he screws up his eyes & crab-claws his fingers in the saltic air

& Malthe crab-claws & catcalls:

boi-yeee!

yþ am sick of it.

but now puppy or no, heartbreak or no, this gangsta COL: The Tropic raps about some bills rolled in his hand. he eyeballs their hollow core & there appears a kaleidoscope picture of him & his *many ladies*, hwa kick their heels in the air & dazzle away into space

& he does his *signature move*:

below his neck he does a full-body boogie & lopes sideways æt the camera, sidles his Nike(™)s *one over them other* & his head glides in straight on a rail & he stares: one eye drilled COL GANGSTA æt the world

he reaches the lens & cocks his head & points his other eye COL GANGSTA across his nose æt the watching world, daring it to mock …

… & Malthe jumps off his chair & tries the *signature move*, he boogies like a flailing muppet across the carpet, uncoordinated & high, & the floorboards joggle beneath him

then, out of breath: *ok, let's hit it,* & we laugh & exit the house.

we trot behind the garage & Malthe retrieves the spliff from its cinder block void.

he sparks & sucks, & yþ reach & toke & yþ say:

yþ do not in fact hate it.

Malthe accepts myn manner of sprecan. he is not rude if he does not look æt me.

hate what?

that thing. that video, that song.

yþ ask, *hwat about þu?*

Malthe looks across his yard. he turns to me æt the sound of Mōdor's car in the drive, now here to pick me up from hire shopping, & yþ know hwat he will say, a break from all we stand for:

I fucking love it.

- þ -

yþ am Eldric. yþ am talking to Tony.

yþ have given him pause.

Your own months?

he is rarely provoked from his hooded lair

not 'months,' yþ cweþe. *'synodics.' yþ will share them, of course.*

on cloudic days Tony's office smells lic moss & mushrooms & tea. tis comforting.

Tony cweþeþ,

And you feel this is necessary?

yþ sigh. we have been over myn motivations.

yes. for yþ am Seer: a verbal savant—

Whoa, back up, Robert. You got a D in Spanish, remember? Spouting Old English doesn't change that. Tell me your thought process.

'Ænglisc,' yþ correct, ignoring also his lapse of myn required address, that Tony in the normal course indulges as healthy *crisis exploration*, in obvious

affront to Mōdor & the male parent, hwa pay good money, *good money*, they remind anyone with ears—

yþ cweþe,

the Bosworth yþ befæl great cann.

Tony's eyes twinkleþ.

Ah! Yes, he cweþeþ. *The book of Old English. The one that gives insight.*

yþ sough. we have been over it.

Tony looks over his glasses æt me & yþ nod & cweþe slowly:

gea. yþ as Seer wish to impart all yþ see. Ænglisc is but a phase.

it seems not important & so we are silent.

at last Tony cweþeþ,

I'm concerned for your feelings of isolation, Eldric.

yþ shrug.

I think you might try to expand a little more. In other ways. Can we talk about that?

sure, yþ cweþe.

certain, yþ self-correct.

- þ -

yþ am Eldric. yþ know of *strabismus* & esotropic eyes because Malthe once patiently told me.

never æt school—was the promise we made the day we first swam together the stoner pond—but this morning we are, we are ever so high æt school.

the lockers chunk open & slam; the junior-senior corridor is a gallery of shadow & steel noise—warmly rebuffed by walls of raw brick—brightly rejected by travertine floor—

second study, reminds Malthe, & trudges along to his locker. yþ turn to myn   locker & fondle its dial.

as usual the Cool Kids cluster down Malthe's locker's way. the hall is a tunnel & there they (hwa include the *cheerleader*, Rebecca) cluster. yþ keep myn eyes forward, but of course they see him:

ay Left-eye! hey Martha!

tis always the same. on a normal day Malthe will ignore & turn to his locker, zip-twist his dial & things will quiet down & we will make fun of them together later.

but today will not be normal. there is an unnatural pause & yþ hear a sneaker *squeak*—

& all lips in the hall are quiet & yþ grasp tis Malthe hwa squeaks, hwa is about to do The Tropic's famous *signature move*, that all the world knows *freaker's been practicing it,* yþ þence

& he *does it,* his back to me, his audience the cluster, his audience Rebecca:

Malthe crab-claws his hands

he full-body boogies

he shuffles æt the cluster

his sneakers squeak & clamber

one over them other;

he glides his head along

straight on a rail

though yþ see from behind yþ know he stares them down COL GANGSTA with his own tropic eye

& then it is over & the sound of the world returns.

nice dance, fruit, cweþeþ the crutched splint-footed one they call Sean.

yet there is Rebecca hwa is *smiling,* a sun behind clouds: hwanne the one they call Leif sees this he claps his hands & steps forward & tries said *signature move* on his own:

but he trips on his own foot in the shuffle—

he rights himself—

& they are all laughing: the one they call Frankenstein, the Humpty-Dumpty figure they call just *dickhead*: the echoes bounce along travertine, hammer softly down brick corridor walls & then all are laughing. Malthe does it again - nails it

my MAN!

a hi-five to Malthe from the tall one called Frankenstein.

Left-eye, you cool, you cool!

their approval blooms & stops æt me where yþ stare

not you, freakshow!

yþ snap myn eyes back to dialing.

ay, you—FREAKSHOW!

Frankenstein points, his finger tracing a trajectory down the hall æt me

NOT YOU!

- þ -

yþ am Eldric. yþ am Asex?

at second study Malthe is waiting to go out & smoke in the trees behind the Dumpster(™)s. he is waving me in but he has news:

hey, that girl—

yþ know hwone he means.

that girl said she wants to talk to me. to us.

Rebecca has deigned tight polite smiles to now in myn social career. sche is friends with everyone, yet in varying degrees.

she said the Music Annex—

that is a wing over & we traipse the macadam past faculty cars to a girl— a *cheerleader*—hwone we both apparently secretly like yet of hwone we have never sexily spoken.

& sche is right there outside: sche hops off the brick planter wall & comes æt us, smiling:

hey-o. hi!—

—sche ever so shyly waves æt me:

oh m'god, Eldric! is that it? is it 'Eldric?' wow! phew!

sche runs her finger down myn sternum & yþ heart that sche gets me, sche *gets* myn whole Goth þing, a label that does not describe me but that yþ accept.

how are you? both of you? when was the last time we talked? didn't you so LOVE that time at Sturbridge?

sche looks æt Malthe, æt me

don't you remember? wow, I do.

twas years ago, but we remember.

wasn't that a great field trip?

was it? it was—somehow—now—recalling the time hwanne Malthe was just a cross-eyed beat-down nobody *from Holland or some shit* & yþ was someplace hushedly *on the spectrum* behind doctor's office doors.

yþ glance æt Malthe, hwose brows tent up in the middle, hwa wears a lopsided leer yþ have not seen before that shows most of the teeth in the left side of his mouth.

Rebecca continues, though yþ do not hear

sche pulls it all together & we are spellbound:

with nothing but taffy & rainbows & Popsicle(™) sticks sche weaves the history of *Us* & we follow hire cues, we blink æt hire wide hwit eyes, hire bright symmetrical teeth, hire pink glossed lips with their hint of glitter; of course we know hire; we have always known hire …

… and anyway, I've been meaning to catch up with you for so - long!

hwa could ever deny.

so listen Malthe?

Rebecca cweþeþ it correct: *malt-uh*, not *Martha*. myn ears tingle again; yþ wonder if yþ am really here.

Malthe, wow: YOU have gotten, like, so - big!

sche winks æt me though: yþ am still here.

Malthe, dju know what a lot of people think?

sche cocks hire head. myn ears blaze.

Malthe: a lot of people think:

sche hearts hire hands together æt hire clavicle, & butterfly-pops the reveal:

that YOU are the next BOO!

yþ take a step back. yþ know exactly not hwat sche means, yet this yþ do know: that we are the Bobwhites—*Go, Bobwhites!*—& that Boo Bobwhite is alive on hardwood between the months of Blot & Hreþ—& the rest of the year æt random bakesales & carwashes—& that otherwise he is dismembered in hulking furric pieces on hangers in the Athletics office, his vacant eyes covered with the same pair of giant phoney Ray-Ban(™)s he dons hwanne he walks the earth & a Bobwhite sinks a three.

Rebecca pokes Malthe in the chest—

Malthe. Listen, Malthe: this is important. Sean is <u>out</u>! He just broke his <u>foot</u>! He's out for the season!

sche has him by the shoulders. sche shakes him a little.

and I have had a vision!

he is liking it, yþ can tell. the shaking

it is this!

YOU are our guy! YOU have got the moves!

Rebecca makes the power play:

do it for US!

Malthe's lopsided leer grows brighter. he cweþeþ not a thing, but he blinks, for Rebecca has presented him both a challenge & a failure scenario. yþ see that he knows this.

Rebecca sees too; sche smiles, goes in, plants a soft one on Malthe's jawbone.

will you think about it?

sche draws back. he nods, but his half-leer is now strained.

aw, thanks, M.

then it is over. *see you in class*, breathes sche, & picks up hire bag from the planter & slides back where sche came through the glassic pull doors.

we stand a full minute, Malthe & yþ, awaiting a vision that will not reappear

then we trip across the parking lot to the Dumpster(™)s behind Vo-Ag wing.

there we toke & huddle behind an iron brown smelly stele flank & in the warmish orange-leafy breeze yþ am ever so, ever so very high

& though yþ am at that moment more in like with Rebecca than yþ have ever been with any girl yþ feel yþ must clear the air of hire preposterous suggestion.

tis indeed a lunatic concept: Malthe in full *Boo*, prancing the sideline

& doing disco rolls with his furric hands & pointing *John Travolta* æt the First National Bank scoreboard.

tis incorrect & yþ so cweþe in our solemn shared manner:
dude:
yþ pause, for tis the pause that lends solemnity
dude: 'One must put up barriers, to keep Oneself intact.'

but Malthe does not hear. he has been dealt a challenge scenario & he knows it & he looks like he has choked on a roll of Sweet Tart(™)s

& second study is almost over & yþ seriously have to piss.

on Wodnesdæg Malthe signals that yþ may not want to attend his tryout, & of course he is right.

it's stupid, he mumbles. *just to get her off my back*, he mumbles.
yes, yþ affirm.

- þ -

yþ am Eldric. yþ am Ink. yþ am Island.

tis Sæternesdæg næht in Ærra Yule. now Mōdor & the male parent let me take the car out. yþ draw into the crowded lot & park behind the gym.

it has lately snowed. the gym windows glow, & yþ feel the noise & excitement from inside the car. yþ might not get out. yþ might not go in.

yþ check myn hær in the fold-down. yþ have clumped it; yþ have teased it. myn platform boots push myn knees to the dash. yþ drove both scrunched & forward-leaning & myn back hurts a little.

tis important, this næht. yþ am here by Malthe's special invitation, the *Friends and Family* ticket.

They give us these, cwæþ he one second study. *If you want*, he cwæþ, & handed me the packet.

yþ might not get out. yþ might not go in.

yþ descend from the car. yþ fasten myn mantle. yþ walk on. yþ walk around. clusters, couples & family groups fall back as yþ pass. there is chatter. yþ ignore from the dark:

nice CAPE, weirdo.
ay MARILYN! AY, SCISSORHANDS!
yþ join the traffic & round the corner.

there the glass doors are propped open by the swing-arms. yþ hear the crowd in the hallway & the band from a deeper layer inside, where the doors of gym proper are open to the squeaks & the slaps on the hardwood where the teams warm up.

there is squeeze & crush to get in, but *yþ*: yþ am poison, oil on water; they spread to make way. yþ am blæc jellyfish, roiling ink from squid: yþ am one not Goth hwa beareþ yet burdens of Goth: yþ am *Harlequin,* yþ doeþ the hǽr, weareþ the platform boots, the guyliner, the lipstick of woad: they will not accept me but they *shall see me …*

Heya, Bobby. Nice getup.

yþ present myn ticket to the taker. he grins up & yþ see with surprise the gap in the teeth of Stash, *Head Custodian,* out of his coverall & duded up in street clothes.

tis Eldric. yþ am Eldric.

Whatever. Nice to see ya.

tis everyone's nǽht out. yþ passe inside. there is strident cymbal activity inside the gymnasium doors & yþ tower in the brightness in time to see Boo do a full split on the gleaming maple between bopping blue skirts. then falleþ silence.

& then there are stares,

& then the cheerleaders take up most quick & the noise rises to normal & yþ go in.

the foldaway bleachers are unspooled & they all seem to know me:

How's the air up there, Bobby?

Look: it's Count Bobby!

—so cweþaþ the prosperous, glowing faces hwa look ǽt myn ticket & hand me along to myn spot ǽt half court. they make much room for me; they scoot wide around me; yþ have space for myn hǽr to its tips, all sides & behind.

Boo's split was the end of the warm-up show & he & Rebecca & the non-Rebecca cheerleaders mill in conference on the sideline. Boo reaches a shaggic mitt & cocks open the front of his neck & Malthe's sweaty eyes & forehead glint out from within. the band falls silent & the First National Bank scoreboard ticks 00:00:00 with a loud hornet klaxon.

the ref whistles, the warm-ups are over; the players take their last shots & trot back to the sidelines as the balls bounce silent one by one by one.

yþ wave but guess that Malthe cannot see me.

yþ see that he has added his own touch to the Boo suit, pasting Boo's left pupil ever so markedly inward & tropic.

- þ -

yþ am Eldric. yþ am Pacifist?

the ref is eating a peach, a peach in Ǽrra Yule. he spits the peach pit in a towel & wipes off his hands.

then we are ready for tip-off. the ten of them take the court & in the center is Frankenstein & a *visitor* even taller with acnefied shoulders.

the ref looks up & leans in & cheeps the whistle pursed between his lips & flips up the ball & it pends an instant high in space;

Frankenstein bests acne visitor & delivers the ball direct to Leif's spread waiting fingers;

the crowd whoops & growls; Coach Kane's face turns red; the game has begun.

things unroll ever so fast. the duo Leif/Frankenstein are the stars. Frankenstein is boxed in by acne visitor until fouled or taking his shot, that he either makes or that falls to where Leif is ready & waiting for down n dirty combat. then it all repeats on *de-fense*. through it are whistle cheeps & the shouts of Coach Kane & in certain interstices the band & Boo, Rebecca & the non-Rebecca cheerleaders spell it all out

& in these brief moments yþ believe not myn eyes, though believe them yþ must:

Malthe as *Boo* is a being unknownst to me.

he is *leaping*; he is *spinning*: possessed by some trickster spirit he mimes & he mimics, enthralling us all:

if dickhead on the drums goes:

bmp-tsst, b-dmp-dmp-tsst

& Boo *walks that way*,

strutting & disco-rolling his mitts:

tis:

a travel

if Boo mimes the infamous time in 8th grade gym Malthe whiffed a pass,

if he makes a circle with both arms,

closes said circle, bends æt the waist

& gazes after a phantom basketball,

& inside-joke hilarity ensues,

tis:

out of bounds

if Boo whips out phoney giant Ray Ban(™)s from a pouch on his person;

if he dons them, crosses his arms,

bends back æt his waist,

& jacks his foam beak up & down,

tis:

a field goal,

or similarly,

if Boo whips out the phoney giant Ray Ban(™)s from a pouch on his person;

if he dons them,

& lies down on the court with his mitts behind his head like he toma el sol,

tis:

extra point on free throw

through it the crowd's laughter & applause ripple across hardwood from cinder block walls

& yþ ask mynself: *is it really myn same friend?*

it goes on & then yþ am startled tis the half

we are winning. Rebecca & Boo & the non-Rebecca cheerleaders take the court & do brief magic to the Bobwhite fight song while the world gets up to pee & to smoke

then Rebecca & Boo & the non-Rebecca cheerleaders retire to the sideline for a break.

Boo's head is between his mitts & Malthe's head pokes from his shoulders. dickhead lifts to the officiating table a matte blæc boombox, hooks the PA & tunes in time for *station identification* æt Ninety-Eight One: *The Hit Star* & then: The Tropic's bright brass chord explodes & a vocal contingent stomps its feet on the bleachers

Do it! they clomp. *DO IT, DO IT, DO IT!*

someone cranks the PA

the song—even tired, even *so last summer*—sounds almost quite delicious in the big space; even the old ladies know it & swivel their hips in the stands

so Malthe cannot rest. he cannot ignore hwat some of them want & the rest are curious to see. he puts on his head & trots out as Boo mid-court & someone *chunks* the breakers & cuts off all lights but one, leaving him spotlighted & reflected in the maple hardwood angelfire:

he dances, he does the *signature move*, & then he remains, & bobs & disco-points some more

& still yþ believe myn eyes na

& our side goes wild & tis then yþ notice

how could yþ not notice?

the stillness in the frenzy that is Sean; his splinted foot cocked off the hardwood, standing in shadow æt the corner of the bleachers like he has just come in from the cold

& maybe he has

looking like he is alone

looking with a clench-jaw smile æt Boo moonwalking off the court & waving his mitts over his shoulders æt the adoring crowd.

yþ see Sean there & the spell of the evening evaporates some.

the lights come up & suddenly Sean is swinging like he has jumped up out of the ground & Boo is swinging back, pushed back on his heels, flailing like a blæw & hwit Sasquatch.

stop FUCKING MY GIRLFRIEND! shouts Sean, swatting & flailing.

Boo rips off his head & throws it æt Sean.

I'm NOT YOUR GIRLFRIEND! shouts Rebecca. *LEAVE US ALONE!*

THAT was The Tropic with last summer's hit, 'Tain't Nuff Lipstik n tha World' blares the DJ

We're not DOOING ANYTHING! shouts Malthe.

AT POLLARD TOYOTA, WE TAKE THE TIME TO blareþ Ninety-Eight One: The Hit Star

& Sean is dirty, he knows the secrets of Boo, he seizes the neck-rim of the Boo-suit with his left hand & punches Malthe with his right as by now the bench is clear & Rebecca is crying

& YÞ:

yþ now know why yþ have been here bidden: yþ spy beneath the scrum Sean's jockey-socked splinted foot

yþ stonde: yþ see below me the bleachers like stairs.

yþ gladden yþ have mynself shod with platforms both towering & steely. yþ spread wide myn mantle: yþ am become wærloga, blæc octopus.

yþ hear myn own cry

NO MONEY DOWN blares Ninety-Eight One.

LOOK OUT! shouts dickhead.

yþ thonder down the bleachers & fly unto Sean.

whadda YOU want, freakshow? he shouts, & squirms from Coach Kane. *think ya can take me?*

& then yþ have his arm.

SEQUOIA! COROLLA! RAV4! ZERO PERCENT INTEREST AND NO MONEY DOWN!

& then stomp his foot.

OOOH says the gym, & Sean is on the floor with his knee in his face, now holding said jockey-socked foot most tightly

ALL DEALER STOCK!

dude, are you SICK? shouts Malthe.

yþ turn now & see Malthe with the lopsided leer showing most of the teeth on the left side of his mouth

only now the lopsided leer is stark.

WHY the fuck'd you DOO that? he shouts.

IT'S TIME TO GET POLLARD!

why the fuck'd you even COME?

yþ reach forward & hug around the Boo suit

—for qualified buyers and lessees. offer includes destination charge—

so he not go away

—excludes tax, title, registration and fees—

EWW, cweþaþ cheerleaders.

—listed rebates and incentives—
aw, c'mon, really? cweþeþ Kane.
—packages or accessories offered at time of purchase—
FORFEIT! FORFEIT! FORFEIT! chanteþ visitors.
—all inventory subject to prior sale—
I will fucking KILL YOU! screameþ Sean.
—does not apply to certified pre-owned—
get the fuck OFF, hisseþ Malthe.
—see dealer for warranty details—
& now the cops are here

- þ -

yþ am Eldric. yþ am in Tony's wait-room.

yþ hear the male parent through Tony's office door:
beCAUSE!

yþ look æt Miss Reception, hwa lookeþ down æt her work & there writeþ most placid.

NO! cweþeþ Mōdor.

tsh-shhh, cweþeþ Tony, and mumbleþ most quiet, until the male parent's voice riseþ again.

Why, if the district will pay for it, Margaret? The DIStrict will PAY for it. OK, see? We've got that.

Shuh. Time out. OK? Shuh, cweþeþ Tony.

they mumble some more.

Mind if I turn on the radio?

Miss Reception is looking æt me.

Little noisy in there, sche cweþeþ.

yþ know hire. sche goeþ to our church.

na, yþ cweþe simplic.

sche switcheþ on a tidy blæc radio to music. of course tis The Tropic, hwa is charting new ballade.

yþ try not to listen to the door, yet listen yþ do
I know. I KNOW. But MILitary?
Not military. It's called Pathway, yþ hear.

Miss Reception is sprecan:
So Bobby, you're—Goth? Is that what you do?

sche is smiling. sche pointers me up and down with her pen, indicating myn hær & myn boots, myn full blæc attire.

sche is trying to be nice.

yþ am one not Goth hpa beareþ yet burdens of Goth, yþ cweþe.

Excuse me?

yþ accept the label, yþ cweþe.

Oh. Well, is it a lot of work?

yþ sprece na.

sche goeþ back to her work.

yþ close myn eyen & listen to the radio. in myn mind yþ can see The Tropic trip through his new video, his hwit shirt fleogan æfter.

yþ þence about Malthe. about hwanne they all crossed thire eyen in 6th grade, mocked his Adidas(™) & his *Yertle the Turtle* & his Danespræac. hwanne Malthe became *Martha*, hwanne the leoht fleogon fro his eyen.

hwa was a freond in þose dæg?

now we sprecaþ na. yþ know na hwat he doeþ. yet yþ have heard lic fact that he, Lief, Frankenstein & others went wiþ Rebecca æt hire parents' condo æt Okemo during Yule break, & was champagne & private outdoor hot tub æt þider yon condo.

hwa was Malthe's freond in old dægen?

the people behind the door murmur on now quietly, & Tony's voice riseþ: *alRIGHT?*

the door openeþ & Tony is there. Miss Reception turneþ down sound.

Robert, Tony cweþeþ most soft. *C'mon in.*

yþ stonde na.

Robert.

Eldric, yþ cweþe.

Robert?

El-dric.

ROBERT, come in here, the male parent calleþ. *No more 'Eldric.' We're all done with Eldric.*

Yes, please, Robert, calleþ invisible Mōdor. yþ hear that she weepeþ. *Just come in here and talk.*

Tony lookeþ æt me. He snappeþ his fingers lic he just remembereþ something.

You know, I keep meaning to tell you, Robert, he cweþeþ. *Did you know? The French also invented their own months.*

really? yþ cwæþe.

Yah. Months, days, weeks. The whole shebang.

yþ feel yþ blinke tears.

Yah, it didn't work out too good.

yþ sniff & yþ feel most heavy. yþ feel lic yþ can na stonde.

C'mon, cweþeþ Tony. *We'll talk about it.*

Miss Reception sougheþ. sche putteþ down her pen.

yþ stonde, & yþ go in.

Boom

MARGOT DOUAIHY

On the sidewalk was a dollar bill. *Boom*, said Kevin. It was green and crumpled, and anyone else would have thought *leaf*, but Kevin was a man who noticed things. He picked up the dollar and spent it on a lottery ticket which won him $10,000 in cash. A week later Kevin boarded a plane from Tampa to Brazil where he joined a canoe trip through silver water. While paddling, Kevin saw a snake sunning itself on the shore. It was huge, this snake, easily the circumference of Kevin's head. Kevin paddled closer. Against the advice of the smiling Tour Guide, Kevin left the canoe to meet the snake on the warm, gritty sand. For one minute, man and snake locked eyes. The Tour Guide sweat so hard his skin blistered; his face, no longer smiling, was striped with terror. But Kevin was not afraid of being bitten. For once Kevin had no fear at all. *This snake is different*, he thought, *one of a kind*! Kevin—often called a scrub by his ex-wife—also felt like he was one of a kind, when he wasn't worrying about his IT job, work he loathed with a fiery passion, the cursing and complaining employees who threatened Kevin when their computers crashed. Sure enough, this snake was special. As Kevin approached, the serpent opened its large mouth and sang a glorious aria in a language Kevin understood. The Tour Guide fainted and the viper disappeared into thick brush, as elegantly as a penny sinks into a wishing well. Though Kevin left the shore and left the country, the snake's song lived on, like dawn reverberating under eyelids after a bumpy night flight.

Kevin returned to Tampa with a sense of purpose he had never known. He quit his IT job and toured neighborhood after neighborhood, then every city along the coast, snatching snakes from pools, pipes, gutters, lawn furniture. Never once was Kevin bitten. He wore snakes like scarves, hoisted serpent tridents. *Real Life Snake Charmer*, headlines declared. Twenty years later, in the dizzying bazaar of a pink city, Kevin noticed a large tank surrounded by light, in the center, a snake. That slither. That skin—wet black as a startled eye. It inched close to the glass and Kevin knew: *My snake!* Kevin belted the aria he had heard performed years earlier by the enchanted viper. He lifted the tank's lid, lowered his hands. *Boom.* Stunned creases in the onlookers' faces spelled horror. The snake's eyes changed in no perceptible way, how a hustler might bluff his next move. The snake launched onto Kevin and snapped his head clean off. As Kevin's hands draped the corner of the glass, his knuckles twitched with the dance of life leaving. In the tank hovered a reptile who could not talk let alone sing, a snake ordinary in every single way, except for inside its belly, like a prayer inside a puff of incense-smoke, a charming man's lips were pursed wildly and forever in *Boom.*

THE BARGAIN

ELEANOR STERN

After Jacob's car plunged into Bayou St. John while I slept through Sunday morning, I felt the world wear through in spots. I knew Jacob had traveled to the other end of one of those holes, where the dead people go. Anyone might fall in as Jacob had. I saw the holes on the road along the Bayou. At intersections, in a drawer of kitchen knives, in the doctor's office. Sometimes a new one would crowd into my peripheral vision and I'd wonder why, wonder what could be dangerous about a pillow or a park bench. And, guarding each of these holes, I saw a black and shaggy creature. Shadows of something hidden. Each one waved when I passed, then used its fingers to grab hold of the hole's borders and stretch it wider to lure my mother and father and friends who did not see these tunnels to nothing.

I'd hoped they would not appear when I moved to the new city. To do research, I explained to friends, on the failed revolution at the end of the last century. This was a cold and clean place without the hot gasp of decay you felt in New Orleans. In the end, after I moved, I did still see the holes on the cold sidewalks. Still, the newness of the place distracted me and loneliness kept to the edges. At first each conversation in the foreign language, with the man who sold me my coffee or with Tom on the landing, drained and excited me. And at first Jacob's absence was a presence in itself. I'd see a huge dog or an old man singing to himself in the library, and for a moment I would think, "I'll tell Jacob about that." Then the other side of my brain would slap and scold: not possible. This constant shock of remembering felt warm and alive on my skin.

Then while I looked elsewhere his absence turned into only an absence. Now the loneliness. My closest thing to a real friend is Tom from upstairs, who caught up to me in the dilapidated lobby in October and said, "I think you are new in the building?" A nice guy, Tom, but someone I wouldn't have looked twice at back home. Always lifting weights somewhere and coaxing me to come and take shots with him of that liquor they all drink here that makes me feel I've got motion sickness.

It's the weekend and I wander to tire myself out until blisters blossom on my toes. More than usual today I see holes in the walls of the world and I cannot possibly warn all the hundreds of people who pass so close to them without a glance. A mother nearly pushes her bulky stroller into one. The hole swims in the middle of the avenue's rush, and she steps forward, then pulls back just in time while a truck growls down. What I need is a fresh distraction. The quick medicine of a person to touch, and my name coming from a new mouth. I hear my mother's voice as if we're on the front porch drinking coffee: "Are you ready for something like that?" Well, if not, I'm still going to do it. In the end, the whole seducing bit is so easy that I consider backtracking and running back to my apartment downstairs. I had not expected it to work, at least not so quickly.

 "Sorry to bother you." I shuffle sweaty on his old doormat. "Have you got a hammer I could borrow?"

 "Claire!" Tom spreads his arms. "I've got one somewhere in this mess! But come in first! Have a drink, it has been weeks and weeks, my friend!"

 I see no mess. Tom's apartment smells of cleaning supplies as usual and shines raw as a plucked chicken, without the soft fuzz of clutter I've cultivated over my identical rooms. I accept the mug he hands me and settle on the worn sofa, breathing the chemical clearness of the liquid in the mug, the room itself. Tom's apartment, like him, offers solace in solidity. The floor flat underfoot and the countertops hard enough to hurt at the corners. The holes-to-nothing dirty my peripheral vision but I keep my eyes on Tom. I do not scoot away when he sits down, and as he shifts closer with a warm exhale I feel static pull us together by the hairs on our thighs.

 I ramble about my research, and he cries, "You are my smartest friend!"

 I feel a gush of affection at the same time that I reply, with a touch to his bicep, "And you are my strongest friend, aren't you?"

 When he reaches to refill my glass I raise it and brush the calluses on his hand. His arms bristle from his tank top with an ostentatious rush of muscle, his hair stands at attention from product and the sheer force of masculine aspiration. I have not had more than one drink since soon after Jacob died—that night on Frenchman Street, all control washed away. I swore not to do it again and then found an excuse to research a city on the other side of the world. So I register little as I step into Tom's bedroom. Only that it smells like lavender alongside ammonia, and that the bed's made so neatly that I have to tug the blankets two-handed to get beneath them.

I lift Tom's shirt and nearly cry. Under the logo-stamped cotton his belly bulges sweet and inquisitive from carved hipbones. That quiver of pale softness, only visible when naked, blinks from the center of a body otherwise as clutterless as this apartment. In a panic of protectiveness I roll him over, push him down onto his back and place my knees on each side of his waist.

At the sight of Tom's belly, a vulnerability exposed to the air, I see a hole widen behind him. A creature grins while it paces the entrance, hungry or just bored. My knees tighten around Tom while I imagine his muscle-busy limbs heaped in the bloody bedroom corner—bones peeking out on the ends, and on top the jiggling half-peach of his stomach. Tom does not know how he's moments from a fall.

He sits as best he can under my body's clutch and reaches into the bedside table drawer. What is the man doing? I think, and then—Oh! I understand, lean over and lay a hand atop his.

"Do not have worries," I say. I feel the falter in my tipsy fluency. "I am on the medicine." This is a lie. My birth-control packet stayed in my purse half-finished after Jacob's accident. I did not imagine it was possible to house a child in my frayed self. Now, Tom squirms beneath me, and I see it is possible, in fact, it's my obligation—Tom lives in peril. My only friend, the only person in months to touch me for longer than an incidental moment. Some part of him can rest safe and grow in me, and I can watch it day and night.

Tom withdraws his hand from the drawer. He nods with great solemnity and bites my neck as if he has just grown teeth and does not know yet how to use them. Nobody's mouth has touched that bit of skin since Jacob's. As Tom lifts his hips to press into me I expect pain and blood—a liquid rush as he dislodges memories frozen somewhere in my pelvis. For a moment I await a torrent of tears. But if any memory remains in my body it stays frozen. So I press myself down until it really does hurt, and then I count through the steps of the task. It's quick and enjoyable like a shower before bed. After, Tom smiles at me.

"You are welcome to stay over," he says. Good—now I can stay here on my back, and though putting my feet in the air is not an option I can at least keep my knees upright. If Tom thinks it odd that I lie there on my back and make hills with my knees under his itchy blanket, and that I scoop his huge head onto my shoulder's safety, he says only, "Good night." We both sleep well.

I wake to rain and slip out of bed to bathe before leaving for the university. Tom says, "See you later," from beneath the blankets and the weight of sleep. My eyes dart to that place under the covers where I know he stores his stomach. I did not lift the blanket to check for it when I woke, though I imagined it gashed and spilling geode-like with organs. On the stairs I step lightly so as not to creak the neighbors awake, and I see a hole hover between the step on which I stand and the landing. A creature drowses at the entrance. In my apartment, the usual black gaps block the windows and deepen in the shower floor. Each of these, too, guarded by a languid shadow-thing.

Rain flicks the windows and the sky weighs night-gray at seven in the morning. The huge metal tub, this cheap apartment's blessing, envelops me in still heat. Outside people probably slip in the rain and skid off the road. The creatures in my apartment must envy their higher-ranking friends, outside gathering chaos like sun-hot blackberries.

I pulled a crazy woman's trick back there. It's not as if I don't know. But here I lie in hot water, feeling so sane I could screech it. I've always crossed my arms and hunched in self-defense at the very idea of pregnancy, the notion that someone could live so near to the tricky place where I eat and breathe. Even with Jacob, I amused myself imagining a baby half-him and half-me, but I couldn't think about housing it in my own cavity. I could not be trusted—I might turn around too fast or cough violently or give in to an unsafe craving as I always did.

But I had been stupid. Jacob sank into the bayou while the mansions beside him slept behind their wooden shutters. Jacob, whose very breath had smelled of safety to me. And all along I was the safe one, and he was the one who'd dropped away into an emptiness. He was only a minor prize, probably, for the creature who waited to yank him over its threshold: young, tragic, but not so very large or strong or famous. Since then I'd goad my own selfishly alive body in every mirror.

Now a solution. Now a chore. I'd use this aliveness I had somehow managed to hoard, would offer up the safe spot in the core of my body as protection for some little almost-living lump. My child can keep me company. Its ears will echo with my breath. And poor Tom, so soft, can make a child and keep it in me: a bit of him for safekeeping. Those cold spaces in the air will not snatch someone who hides beneath the lining of my skin.

Under the water I lay my hands over my stomach. In my mind: Tom and me in a field somewhere. Our bellies creep over the tall grass, his fearful as a rabbit. Mine a tower, clanging if you dared to hit it. I do not go to the library today. I lie in the cooling water and listen to rain, and when it stops, I sleep there in the bath.

Of course, I had no way to know yet if that first attempt had worked. Two weeks I distract myself. At dawn's first glow each day, I press my face into the pillow, and I write and rewrite a contract with the creatures. I get a chance to carry a child, a bit of me and a bit of poor Tom, and he'll come to no harm just yet. In turn I will not disrupt the creatures while they go about their business. I will not go looking for Tom until I have, at least, waited long enough to see if I am pregnant. If I take the test at the end of two weeks and it comes back negative I can dash up to his door, strip naked and knock, but until that moment I will wait, give the creatures their space. And, I swear to those shadows, while they polish the entrances they guard, that I'll develop no more attachments in this city. Tom I've befriended and it's too late. Him, I have already seen naked and will insist on protecting. But I'll learn no other names and will look into no faces on the sidewalk and the tram. Anybody else, the creatures are welcome to pull into their holes and out of the living world, and I can't object.

These constant negotiations cram the space around my brain so much that I hardly read at the library. I hold the books open in front of me and say to the creatures, "Go ahead. Take the old librarian back into your holes. Take the feral cat who walks up and down my block." I stick to my terms by cleaning up my own insides, readying them for the baby. My cigarettes go in the trash; I don't lift the heavy boxes of books off the library floor. When I hear that a man's been plucked from the river just downstream of the city, more rotted fruit than human, I stay still and refuse to make eye contact with the bright-eyed creatures who egg me on from their burrows. Of course I want to check on Tom. Of course in my mind I see him on the edge of mortal injury—he stands there on the riverbank, and his stomach grows heavier and heavier until it tips him head-first into the water. But—"No", I say to the creatures. "This city is a large one. You cannot trick me into fear." A glimpse of Tom on the stairs or in the lobby does not seem too much to hope for, but none comes, and I do not let myself ask why.

I sleep well those two weeks, better than I have since before Jacob died. When I speak to the creatures it feels all at once like conversing in a spiky new dialect and like bargaining with my own dried-out brain, and so I tire out before sundown. I dream about him. Dream that Jacob appears naked and climbs into the metal tub with me, dream that he wakes me up by licking my entire body with a tongue that scraps my skin off and leaves me pinkly unshelled, dream that he's fucking me with my wooden cooking spoon. The next day while I make coffee I take the spoon from the drawer and sniff it. It smells only of jarred pasta sauce.

I used to dream differently about Jacob, not just about sex. When he was alive, we'd study together in my dreams or cook dinner. When he was newly dead, I'd dream of him tapping me on the back at a gathering, maybe his own funeral. He'd jerk his head to say, Let's get out of here. Then we'd go back to our house on Chestnut Street to laugh and eat candy, bags and bags of it. And then a knock or a phone's ding. And he'd have to go very, very quiet, to crouch behind the couch. Fear glowed behind his blue eyes. Like a drowned man he did not even breathe. He was dead, you see, and so could not be seen tasting candy on his own tongue, wearing his own skin and hair. This was against the rules. And I'd wake up, thinking, I hope they didn't get him yet. But I have not dreamed a dream like that in a while.

Then the morning for the test comes. I slept with it on the floor beside my bed, where my feet touch down first thing. The verdict: I'm not pregnant. If my   stomach bulges it comes from the store-bought pastries I've eaten for so many meals while I try not to think about how Tom could slip on his shining bathroom floor and disappear down a hole. I leave the test on the bathtub rim and go to the library. At the regular time and not a second earlier I pack my books up and leave. I buy a buttery pastry outside the tram stop. "See," I say to the creatures, who are lounging in the soft light of evening. "I am not afraid of you. I'll take my sweet time." I brush the flakes of pastry from my sweater and do not look at the other passenger's faces while I ride to my stop. One. Two. One. Two. I keep my pace reasonable on the extra flight of steps from my own floor to Tom's.

Fear rises again in me as I look down at Tom's doormat with its lacy trim. In the delicate holes of that synthetic strip I see mouths of blackness. A breath of anticipation clouds from them onto my ankles. I hold my own breath as I knock. One. Pause. Two. The creatures at their holes stroke their stomachs.

"For fuck's sake," Tom says when he answers, with affection. A few seconds later he's picked me up, my backpack still on, and tipped me onto his bed. Perfectly wrapped again in its blankets. After so much fear I stare at the way he yanks his shirt off one-armed. But there again—the belly—and above Tom's face is the face of a child. Down I lie, this time beneath him with my legs clasped around his hips until I'm numb from knee to ankle. The fat on our stomachs squishes together. One of his arms snakes down somehow around our boundedness, strokes and prods into me, widening my own body into black tunnel. I know what must be done.

"All right," I say to the creatures, in a thought so quiet that Tom with his cheek sticking to mine will never feel it. "I'll make you a deal." And from crannies of the flat—the lacy bit on the doormat, the slick-washed bathroom floor, the wires bare in the kitchen—creatures swarm around my nakedness. One looming thing blurs into hundreds. They trace me all over with their matted hair, breathe their rotten heat over my skin.

"Let me make you an offer. Tom and I for Jacob," I pitch. The creatures suck on their hands and watch coolly while Tom's other hand, the one not between my thighs, squeezes my shoulder. "This man is tall and muscular, better than Jacob really. I know, I know, you're going to take him anyway. Tom is going to die. But when you take him, at least give Jacob back. And I'll make it worth it—I will share myself with you. I am a woman, already full of holes. Let me be your real estate. You'll have a living woman to use for yourself, so much better than those dirty corners most of you guard now. Better than those drawers and nasty ponds."

Tom guides himself into me and I feel sweat squeeze from everywhere. This is the last chance to make myself clear.

"You understand what I am asking," I say, as the creatures begin to wriggle into the crevices of fat and muscle between me and Tom. "A tunnel can go both ways." And the creatures are gone. Except for one. I feel it climb up into me, nudged in with the help of Tom's thrusts. A little thing, striking out alone. I feel construction; lifting and widening the inches between my hips into a space so vast it's no longer space. On the outside I think I look the same. In me, though, gapes a moonless winter night. I grip Tom's chin between my fingers and look at his face while his handsome skin sands my hand with stubble. The eye contact, it seems, does it for him: he yelps and gushes up into the emptiness in me. And I know the creature waits there. Tom, though, falls heavy onto me. Still warm, stomach flattened into mine.

I pull my knees up on either side of the dead man whose weight crushes my chest. I do not look. Instead I think of Jacob, his long neck, his soft waves of hair, his voice that I have spent months not remembering in case it becomes scratched from overuse like a CD. Soon I will not have to worry.

When I can wait no longer I push Tom out of me, how I do not know, and I dress and leave. One. Two. One. Two. I feel no warmth, no dripping between my legs. Only the howl of wind circling in me. I count the steps all the way down, past my apartment and to the lobby, down to the tram station. I ride it to the end of the line and then all the way back. Rush hour commuters with grocery store bags become girls in high heels, then those same girls with hair messily pulled back and half-asleep. I grip the pole with both hands and do not sit even when a teenager totters up on her stilettos to give me her spot. I cannot sit while I am thanking, again and again, this creature that has taken over my body. Already it's calling Jacob back from the other side, from wherever the hole of me leads. Jacob's bloated drowned self will grow again in that emptiness, fingernails and hair and nostrils. He'll lie there just inside the door and when it's time he'll emerge, a reverse-journey never taken before, until him—someone who was loved enough to be brought back from the dead side.

Unless I tease the creature (after all, if he is the new owner of my insides then we must be allowed to joke with one another). Unless, of course, others have done this before me, made this bargain. Unless every mother has traded her body to bring somebody back, and every baby learns to forget the time it fell through a hole in the world and became nothing before it could become a something again. Even now, I ask the creature while I sway in the empty car, is Tom only hunched just beyond what I can see, waiting his turn, for some woman to miss him enough that she makes him her child? The creature stays silent. Teasing me back, maybe, or busy reassembling Jacob.

In any case. Even if others did it first, I feel I have made the woman's discovery by learning to use my body's empty spaces. And just beyond the edge of them Jacob waits. When he falls back out of me, his cry will sound like the one that filled his car as it sank into the bayou, the one I hear in the silence between my breaths. But this time will be different. I will hear it and say, Hello little thing, it's you, it's you.

Untranslated

Farnaz Fatemi

In the silence of my girlhood, spoons
clattered in glasses of tea.

The squeak of the front door
rang out. I was the child

I'd never have, I listened for clues.
I spoke without saying a thing,

made sounds to fill
the spaces. I could see

around everyone, my teeth and eyes
gleamed, face open, a flower,

as if to say to these people,
Speak. Say things I understand.

Their untranslated words thunked
in my head. A cyclist in traffic, whooshing by.

Honking. And wind. Piles of autumn leaves,
feet that crunch them.

Staticky din of English and Farsi
with afternoon fruit and cookies,

my lips mouthing along with them
to pay attention, as I wrote their stories

in my head, rearranged the letters
into meaning. I heard the squished sounds

of a heartbeat in a stethoscope,
pump and thrum.

In the languages
of women I could have been

I felt both lonely and contained.
We were chador-less,

light-skinned. All the women
who disappeared into the silence are inside me,

I pull from the roar of the past.
I make introductions. By which I mean,

I want the foreigner in me
to meet the foreigner in me.

The Practice of Parting Before the Farewell Even Exists

Tyler Dunning

I've undertaken risky behavior: reading in the tub. Seems innocuous, sure, but what an act—to hold and suspend that which you cherish over its own great destructor. I can't recall ever fumbling or dropping a book when liability was involved, but, yet, in the tub it's all I envision—the book falling—which then only increases the likelihood of my recent purchase, Pete Fromm's *The Names of the Stars*, at $16.00, slipping into ruin. (This cover price, embarrassingly, is beyond the range of replacement.) The outcome seems inevitable, mere inches between paperback and water. Yet the calm and the warmth and the Epsom salts all urge me to chase minor delight. To live dangerously. After all, it's been a tough month—

Typical day: Jenene, my partner, wakes groggy, sufferer to my morning energy, and expresses her desire to survey. A recurring practice. I see her, through kitchen window, tiptoeing barefoot from scattered wild-flower seeds to transported dahlias to hopeful sunflowers. She reports back, delighted, with all that the soil has bid. This isn't enough: she takes me, hand in hand, pointing from one seed leaf to the next, one unexpected blossom to another. Wisteria, peonies, poppies—her favorites. Others we're leery of, like the beautiful but invasive hedge bindweed, its angelic white trumpets stemming from a strangling vine below, roses and irises fallen victims to its prey. The sun shines. Cyclists buzz hither and yon. She kisses me.

It's unlike anywhere I've lived, Seattle, the "Emerald City," truly shrouded in green. What's more, this verdant municipality, proven in spring, births such an abundance of unaccustomed flora that I find myself on daily walks, stunned or perplexed by new blooms. A seemingly humdrum bush, from one afternoon to the next, can erupt in vitality—organic fireworks of pink, yellow, baby blue. All this weighed against former cautions of gloom, that the Northwest is better left to those with stable brain chemistry. Well, my sun-browned shoulders say otherwise. The clear skies, honest. And Jenene, she kisses me.

Yet somehow, still, the gray.

I weave in and out of noonday light, dancing to stay in shadow; such gifted radiance feels like mockery when feeling psychologically under the weather. Gray, a near three-week cycle. My old friend. Depression.

Jenene has never experienced me like this, though I've often alluded to the disease as my identity, a serotonin-starved libido my secondary proof. Signs of her concern come through in heightened love languages, like home-made peanut butter cups or heavyhearted eye contact that no cooking could ever rectify. She doesn't know what to do with me.

The solution, I've found, is to wait. Being familiar with this unwanted visitor, its patterns predictable, I then welcome rock bottom so that I can start the recovery process, back toward cerebral stasis. Toward restoration, like a slow build with immediate release. Like a deep dive, the pressure compounding and guiding light fading, wondering how far one can descend before a desperate explosion up for air. Or expiration.

Day five feels like the worst of it. But it's not. Day eight the same. Then nine. And thirteen. I reach great depths. Set personal records. All on a single breath. I've become so adept at the skill, that others have started to seek me out. For example, one year ago I was flown to London to give a talk on the matter—that is, surviving with suicidal tendencies. Truly a milestone in my career. Yet my sharpest memory from the trip belongs to the stanch Romanian brute who chauffeured me from Heathrow Airport to the O2 arena, he enquiring en route about my line of work. I knew it was a mistake to divulge, to adhere to my confessional nature, but I did. I told him I'd be sharing stories about friends I'd lost to self-slaughter and how I often contemplate the same for myself. "Jesus Christ," he said, "do you people just seek each other out? When I start feeling that way, I grab the bull by the horns, take control, and drive its face into the fucking ground. If you're depressed for one day, fine. Two days, fine. But by the third day, it's your own damn fault. Depression is for pussies."

This is the greatest fear for us pussies: to take the cathartic risk of exposing our principal shame and then receiving admonishment in return. Best to stay quiet, I suppose. Best to sequester the hurting to more internal torment. And certainly, best to leave the stable-brained general public to wonder, when such placating silence reaches a fever pitch, what exactly went wrong amidst another surprising swan song—

But they seemed so happy, they'll say. A cute mantra for the uninitiated.

But such outward hostility, jarring as it may be, is rare, and a reminder that not all nationalities are as emotionally sympathetic as therapy-loving upper-class America. My new Romanian buddy did hit something right on the head: we, the depressed, tend to find each other.

We find each other: through paint, through prose, through ceramics, through song—a binding that's borne of artistic inclination. We cling to others stuck to the same rat glue trap. It's comforting. And problematic.

One such difficulty is that in times of need, instead of relying on real-life relationships, we tend to cling to the wrong company, a catch-22 tribe of those who could've commiserated with us but are no longer around to help: the long-since dead. Mine: an author, David Foster Wallace, who took his life ten years ago and, freshly added to the list, a musician, Scott Hutchison, with the same self-concluding end having befallen him only ten days prior to this writing. I look for solace in their work but uncover warnings instead. Take the former, Wallace, the man responsible for the opus *Infinite Jest*, which, when read with a diseased disposition, becomes the most encompassing embodiment of suicidality I've found on the entertainment market—entertainment, the author's own burdensome focal point of paranoia and despair. He gives us this depiction of depression:

It is a level of psychic pain wholly incompatible with human life as we know it. *It* is a sense of radical and thoroughgoing evil not just as a feature but as the essence of conscious existence. *It* is a sense of poisoning that pervades the self at the self's most elementary levels. *It* is a nausea of the cells and soul.

At age 46 Wallace hanged himself, his suicide then becoming the invisible verification stamp, like a Pulitzer Prize, on the book's cover, verification that the hurt you'll find inside is torment approved. We've seen it before: Cobain, Cornell, Elliott Smith, Hemingway, Plath, Woolf, Hunter S. Thompson, Robin Williams. Our romance for the "tortured artist" exponential, but never more so than to a fellow tortured artist.

Hence, my current fixation: Scott Hutchison, found dead on May 10, 2018. I fall into the rabbit hole that is his band, Frightened Rabbit. I listen, I read, I dig. Throughout the band's catalogue you find lyrical allusions to a body suspended over water, then falling, swimming, sinking. And what an act—to hold that which you cherish dearly over its own great destructor. With hindsight on his musical content, though, the current outcome seems inevitable, Hutchison found on the banks of the River Forth. His song lyrics, from 2008, haunt the scene ten years later: *And fully clothed / I float away / (I'll float away) / Down the Forth / into the sea / I think I'll save suicide for another day.*

What scares me most is perhaps the crux of my pursuit: we find each other because we're afraid of each other. Afraid of the shared signs of an ill fate. For example, I think of the first time I learned it was real, self-infliction to a fatal degree, and how in high school my older brother helped carry a casket containing his dead friend. I'd only been running scissors along my forearms until that moment, but then started thinking about knives, firearms, a car left idling in the garage. It's called a "suicide cluster" when one death triggers the next and the next and the next. A contagion. Like a plague, from a graphic novel or a bad M. Night Shyamalan movie. My brother, when reflecting, would recall how his dear dead friend used to look up every word he came across that he didn't know—I do that too—and left me to wonder if that was the first symptom. I still think of death every time I get out the dictionary. Every time I open a book.

The point: we think we're okay, until we're not. Little things, like dictionaries, become these reminders despite whatever we tell ourselves. Take Hutchison, almost exactly four years before his suicide, expressing on a podcast interview, in his charming Scottish accent, a familiar optimism:

> It's not a secret that, you know, I've sort of had brushes with kinda suicidal thoughts. Those are gone. Those are very much mid- and late-twenties [thoughts]. That kinda thing seemed like an option somehow. I think the older I get, of course, I don't think it should be an option. I'm not gonna . . . it's just the way I was thinking at that point in time.

He thought he was going to be okay. He *wanted* to be okay. I want that too, my brain the most stable and reliable it's been in decades. Yet ghosts of these absent artists and friends whisper my way. They say, over and over, *Give it a rest, kid. We did.*

Jenene and I end the day where we began, in bed, less playful. She feels my gray and is apprehensive to ask if I've returned to old ideation, but she does. A brief silence follows—

I've never lied to her. Never will. Instead, I lie supine wishing I could imbue her with all of *Infinite Jest's* 577,608 words. With the infectious laughter that Hutchison left in so many of his interviews. I wish I could introduce her to my tribe—Cobain, Smith, Williams, Thompson—and say, *See, we're going to be fine.* But it's a tribe, as I've said, that comes with a catch.

Instead, Jenene holds me while I struggle through another apology. Because telling her, *Yes, I've been thinking about suicide again,* feels worse than infidelity. A betrayal. As though she, along with everything else that restores grace to my waver, isn't enough.

And that's the underlying transgression, always the first thing people ask about, especially with our recent slew of celebrity suicides: Wasn't the wealth enough? Or the fame? Or, for God's sake, family? Because leaving loved ones behind, that's the great conundrum of it all, the great insult that none of us can wrap our heads around. Why is nothing enough? Why isn't everything enough? If it made sense though, suicide wouldn't occur, let alone be a global pandemic. But love, the very thing people assume the solution, isn't a pharmaceutical. We've turned love into a non-medical means to a medical crisis though, a situation as absurd as thinking love could counteract cholesterol, reverse diabetes, or cure cancer. But love *is* the preventative plea—a request to alter a diet, to get more exercise, to stay on meds. To seek help. Hence, the refusal to change year after year—not the singular moment of execution—is the transgression. The lasting insult.

I tell Jenene yes. I tell her I have been thinking about killing myself. That it's not her fault. That these things come in cycles, and that, like the flu, the sickness will pass. I promise it will pass—

But at what cost? Each night becomes a new weight to the day. A new transfer of my daily darkness into her. It's unsustainable. But like I said, I'm no stranger to the pattern, and I know what comes next. I've got to purge. To get this shit out. I need rock bottom. Looking to the calendar, I anticipate its arrival. My birthday.

I take a steady, deep breath. And sink.

Guest after guest arrives, all bringing what was asked of them: booze. Tequila. Mezcal. Liquid depressants. And we consume, with homemade carnitas amidst caring conversation. My tribe. One that can commiserate. And help. But a birthday is no place to drag my troubles around as an acceptable answer to salutations. So I party properly and save the climax, waiting for everyone to leave before slipping into the tub, rambling to myself in a self-poisoned delirium. Jenene hears, alone in the house, beaconed, afraid, and sits with me. Her on the toilet, me in the tub, as I tell the woman I love the hardest fear that I hold: that in no circumstance does this story end without me killing myself. And Jenene, she kisses me.

I wake up with little recollection of the night before but am steeped in shame, physically sick and emptying my stomach of any remaining toxins. I know I've said things I can't take back. Can't erase. I try to force down a meal before Jenene and I pursue the scheduled delight of winding double lane roads up to Mount Rainier—my birthday present vacation—and the absolute worst thing you can do during a hangover. But I'm free and clear, the depression cycle complete. I reemerge. Safe once more. Freedom from the gray for now.

But, at what cost? Because Jenene is no longer surveying her plants. Tiptoes less carefully amidst the garden. She is holding something. Suspended. Something which she cherishes dearly over its own great destructor. And there is a lack of confidence, or certainty, that wasn't there before, like it's all she can envision—this thing falling—and I know for sure she's afraid that this growing uncertainty will only increase the likelihood of her grip slipping, and that this thing—which no one can seem to properly name or rationally explain or salvage through unconditional love and grit—will pass through her fingers, heavy as the memory of a hand once held, and forever fall beyond any range of conceivable worldly replacement.

I love her. I would never leave her. But I've seen this pattern before: it's the practice of parting before the farewell even exists.

Jezabel's Reformation

Hannah van Didden

She eyed the mop-haired stranger on the doorstep through the cracks in her rockabilly fringe, not saying a word while her cigarette burnt down and his too-bright smile sent multicolored streamers through the house.

"Ding-dong," he sang in a major third, as though she hadn't heard the doorbell in the first place.

She pushed aside the smile-streamers and inhaled from the stick in her fingers, charm bracelet clinking with the movement.

"What are you selling?" hung in a speech bubble from her open mouth.

"The start of your eternal life!"

So began a neat musical routine with rhinestone-studded Havaianas twinkling at her from under his grey robe. When he was done, he offered her his hand, which she didn't take. But she did take out another cigarette.

"I'm Daryl. Your savior," he said in a voice made for radio. "I was in the area, and being my second time round, I'm doing house calls. I am the light you've been searching for."

"Searching?" Her smoke expanded in the space between them like a living fog. "Searching is such a strong word. I might have heard of you, or at least the idea of you."

"I know," he said. "I know everything there is to know about you, Sharma."

"Forget the nametag. The name's Jezabel."

"I knew you were going to say that because I can see into you," he said. "I can literally see what's in your heart."

She crossed her arms over her chest. Her mind flicked through sepia-tinged slides of the brother who drowned, the uncle cornering her in the church quiet room, the never-present parents, and all the cuts ever since. If he could really see her heart, he would see it was bled-out and tough.

"I can predict the future too." He pointed at the stick in her fingers. "Those things'll kill you."

"Anyone could tell me that." She stubbed the last glow of her cigarette into the pot plant by the door. "Anyway, I know your story. If you are who you say you are, you'll have scars on your hands and a hole in your side."

"I am an excellent healer," he said and, after he flashed his pristine palms, he proceeded to tell her about her deadbeat boyfriend and the meaning of life and what was really in yesterday's sausage roll.

She wasn't in the market for an organized god but Daryl had her intrigued, mostly because he reminded her of the fourth incarnation of Doctor Who. And, as he continued to speak, she nodded with the crystallizing knowledge that this was the face she had seen peering in at her through various windows over the course of her adult life, creepy or kind she couldn't decide right then. But the air around them was getting cold.

"You'd better come in," she said. "Tell me more over a cup of tea."

"I'd prefer Jelly Babies."

"I have those too."

"I knew you would," he said.

Jezabel offered her guest the purple leather armchair—the one under the   unconnected lamp that was there for decorative purposes only—and Daryl managed to illuminate the room. She pulled the cotton wool from her ears and the spikes from her words. And she allowed her lips to curve upwards, which cracked the trowelled-on foundation from her face. He told her she looked better without it anyway.

He called around on the following day at a similar hour, and daily for weeks of days after that. He liked to make sure she was secure, that sure she wasn't wasting time on time-wasters. He liked routine; she liked his routine. Her penchants for nicotine, her good-for-nothing boyfriend, and stage make-up fell by the wayside in favor of a new ritual of talk and tea and infant-shaped jubes.

Every so often, however, he would drop a peculiar phrase or look at her in a particular way that rippled her newfound certainty. She'd let him know when this happened, of course. Then he would laugh and she would laugh, and it was as though none of it had happened. He was good like that, the way he restored order to her world, but his constant misdirection was thinning her suspension of disbelief. Even he could see that.

He set out to prove himself by performing a miracle: he presented her with a barbed-wire ball, ostensibly from her chest. He promised to fill the resultant void but, before he could, the barbed wire corroded and he started to break apart right in front of her.

First, a section of his cheek fell away. Then his entire scalp lifted in a pink toupee, revealing metal cogs and electronica. His fingers scrabbled at his skin, struggling to hold the exterior together.

The strangeness of this experience shocked Jezabel back to the subject of his perfect hands.

"The barbed wire was an illusion," she said. "And there never were any scars. Because you're a robot—aren't you, Daryl? But why here? Why me?"

"I'm your brother," he said, "resurrected."

She held her hands to her mouth; his flew to the ceiling.

"After my bionic conversion, I was programmed to come back for you."

"You can't be for real."

"I'm better than real. I can fix everything, and so could you. You can be   converted and, like me, recruit for the eternal. A living miracle. But first, you'll need to let go of what you have."

He approached her with a meat cleaver—did she just see him produce that from his throat?—and she backed away, her face wet with horror.

"Stop it, Daryl! I don't want to be like you."

"You've got no one else. I thought you'd be happy to see me."

"You are not my brother."

"But I could be."

"I don't believe in you," she said, "especially when you can't give me a simple miracle."

"You. Don't. Believe ..." His speech grew shallow, quickening to something akin to hyperventilation.

"More wine, for example," she continued, brandishing a glass. "I could use more wine."

Daryl's torso twisted round and round on itself and, in the inevitable unwind, he corkscrewed through the front window in an explosion of metal and brick and glass, and screeches so guttural that it took a moment for Jezabel to realize she was producing them. His blast-hole formed a wind tunnel in a crow's line to her and, through this, sharp objects hurtled, destroying trinkets, doors, furniture, walls—every object in its path but her.

Then it stopped.

A thick haze coated her eyes. The air reeked of melted hair and plastic. Spot fires lit the corners of the living area. Her survey of the wreckage showed the only unbroken things were in her TV corner with its display lamp and purple leather.

She reclaimed the armchair she'd designated for Daryl and, in the act of sitting, her bottom set off the crackle of a familiar plastic. She retrieved the forgotten packet, withdrew a crumpled white cylinder, eyes searching the spot fires for a suitable light.

By the time Daryl reappeared the next week on her doorstep, pasty-white and stinking of over-fried vegetable oil, Jezabel had remodeled the house.

"You came back," she said.

"Impressed?"

"Surprised."

"You're smoking again."

He looked her up and down, and she did the same to him.

"And you look terrible," she said.

"It can happen when you rebuild."

"What are you doing here, Daryl?"

"I brought your proof."

"Little late, don't you think?"

His open hands showed red welts melted into sweaty rubber.

"And these are fresh," she said, flipping his hands over, and over again. "Painted on, and not pierced through."

"There's this too."

He lifted his robe. Above silver boxer shorts was a view through his middle to the front garden. He'd had a hole fitted to one half of his gut, and condensation congealed in brown blobs between sliding Perspex sheets.

"You can stick your hand right in. Try it," he said.

Jezabel gave the casing a push. Sparking wires and cauterized rubber tumbled out at her. She snatched back her hand with a wince.

He shoved the electronic offal back into its cavity with a pair of tiny tongs. "My man Lucas did say, 'Twenty-four minutes to touch-dry, twenty-four hours for diamond hardness.' So it needs time, but it's clearly a hole in my side. Pretty cool, don't you think?"

"Are you serious?" she said, but he seemed not to hear.

"I can give you what you want now." From the folds of his robe, he presented a booklet and three small bottles. "For you. And you are so welcome."

She crinkled her face and read the bottle labels aloud: "Natural Red Color (Cochineal). Alcohol—175° Proof. Grenache Flavor. What is this?"

"Your very own water to wine miracle." His hands were twitching. Preparing. "This upgrade's just what you ordered. Now say you believe."

Before he had the chance to do his cleaver trick again, she slammed the door in his face.

The ensuing door-banging was largely drowned out by the evening news, ceasing entirely at the eventual release of a corrosive gas she'd built into her security system.

Flashing onto screen was a story about a self-destructive tow truck, the latest in a spate of machine suicides. Footage of the defunct truck being dragged from the lake was shaky; in the background, another vehicle shuddered, its headlights dipped.

This became the when that she considered her treatment of her would-be savior may have been over harsh, that maybe his feelings were based in reality, but they were both practiced at moving on. And this last week she had, really. There was no clear mark of his ever setting foot in her world. Except for the remodeled bungalow, her singed-short hair, her much-upped alcohol consumption. Her gaping heart. But these were ultimately her doing. He had been a catalyst at best. Knowing this brought her to smile.

She lifted her drink to her memories, her bracelet chinking a solo cheers against rum-dulled crystal, and she set about fashioning a new life purpose.

The display lamp suddenly shone bright. A sign. A wonderful, impossible sign! She'd write her manifesto in this very air. It would be a good book indeed—*The Book of Jezabel*, she would call it—and she would convert it to an ebook and distribute it for free. Her book would be so compelling that it would attract disciples and a TV show and multiple other book deals in sixty-nine languages. And after her death, millions of people would bicker about following her teachings to the comma.

But first she would find that Lucas chap and get him on side. Because she could think of a dozen better ways to become a bionic icon than installing X-ray vision and someone else's scars.

Black Escapism

Faylita Hicks

When we finally begin to break,
our bones shattering under the serrated tongue
of a scalpel in our beloved brother's hands,

after knowing our father's steel motive,
weighted ardently upon the strident chords
cocooned in our flightless bodies,

in accordance with the wool laughter
stretched too thinly across our mother's chin, agile
as the buffed legs of any loose muse liquored,

we will itch to taste the sweet vinegar graze of Joy—
a finite whiskey—hurried down our throats. As a deterrent of sorts,
it will roar gloriously into our gut, bubble against our lips

like laughter. A final offense against the defiling hour—
a final defense against the sluggish corrosion of our pitiful outfits,
a final relief to these skins we have become too accustomed to.

Before we are forced to surrender to one of our many kinds of death,
we will let Joy sear every inch where breath once belonged,
until pain is phantom and we stand no more.

South Carolina, 2012

Meredith Doench

My father lost the key more than a month ago. Since then, time has stopped on the old grandfather clock that he claims has been in his family for at least two generations, sometimes more depending on the day you ask him.

Thoughts of the past often mist across my father's eyes, a rheumy caul that signals he's gone back in his mind: "I remember working on this clock with my great-grandpa."

The facts, however, tell a different story; the great-grandfather in question died long before my father's birth and no other living relative remembers such an heirloom. The neurologist warned this would happen—indiscriminate fixations on random objects. As the neurons in my father's brain die, messages misfire, directions re-route, and memories completely fall apart.

Every Sunday evening is the designated grandfather clock winding time— colorful sticky reminders and random lists that line the kitchen counters tell my father so. He stands in front of the towering vessel and opens its coffin-box body to reveal the complicated innards. He pushes the pendulum back and forth. He yanks on the weights. Without the key, its full-moon face and delicate arms remain motionless.

My dad worries that losing the key proves that the neurologist's foreboding diagnosis is correct. He pulls at his shock-white hair that always stands on end and turns over every drawer. He takes apart the refrigerator as objects sometimes turn up lodged between the milk and mayonnaise. He sifts through the vacuum bag until his fingertips are ashen with dust. My father believes that if he can find this clock key, he can prove his neurologist wrong once and for all.

"Where is that damn key," my dad muses, sipping his martini on a stifling hot Tuesday night. In his retirement, he says, every evening feels like a Saturday night. "I never lose important things."

I don't remind him that his misplaced house keys turned up between the dewy heads of broccoli in the grocery produce section yesterday, or that I found his insurance card last week tucked inside the value-size box of Frosted

Flakes.

I try to reassure my dad. "You don't need it."

The kitchen timer's ding interrupts us. "What the hell?"

"It's the reminder bell to change your medication patch."

He's just as surprised as he was 24 hours ago as he shuffles to the kitchen for something he cannot remember. He returns with another martini.

Later, after my father has fallen asleep in his chair with the TV's volume set on blow-your-hair-back, I lounge outside by the retirement community's glowing pool. The cloudless night hosts a near full moon and I let the summer's humidity and heavy heat blanket me. Noise from the televisions in every unit combine to a low rumble. Alone, finally, I pull the object from my pocket that's been gnashing into my hip all day.

I found the clock key jammed inside the garbage disposal. My long fingers reached into the carriage beneath the rubber stopper and pulled up the metal culprit: a terribly mangled and distorted grandfather clock key with its distinctive three leaf clover shaped head. The moment I found it, I knew I would keep it forever—a hard physical reminder of what happened during the long forgetting.

In a few days, I will drive my father to his neurology appointment while we practice random questions as if we are on the game show *Jeopardy*. "Who is the president of the United States?" I will quiz him. "How many hours in one day? What county do you live in? What is your middle name? What years were your children born?" He will stumble on the answers but shine with my encouragement until he sees the inside of the examination room. There, sitting on the padded table with a blood pressure arm cuff buzzing tight, he will tell the doctor that the president of the United States is Osama Bin Laden and that despite the blazing heat, Christmas is only days away. The doctor will nod, as is his way, and ask how the new memory patch medication is working.

"Great," my father will chirp. "Never been better."

The doctor will hand him a blank sheet of paper and a pen. "That's wonderful news. Could you draw me a clock? A face that reads 4:00."

I will watch as my father draws an oblong circular shape and struggle to mark the hour points. The doctor's eyes will warn me not to help as my father produces some sort of clock that looks like it came from the untrained hands of a preschooler.

At the pool's side and drenched in South Carolina moonlight, I silently cry. My tears aren't because in a few days' time my father will forget he lost the key or that he even owned a grandfather clock. My tears are because I won't be able to forget him winding those delicately curled edges of the hour and minute hands backwards, as if it were that easy.

STORYTIME

JESSICA BARKSDALE

At first, it was colors, great blobs of primary colors. Yellow like an egg yolk, not that I knew what an egg yolk was at the time. Blue like a sky in some unpolluted land. Green like a lawn watered by those oblivious to global warming.

Later, large letters from the Latin alphabet lumbered behind me like lost St. Bernard puppies, panting. Sometimes, crowds of vowels surrounded me, lumpen and round. They formed small groups and began to sing.

Consonants clattered by in a cacophony of raucous cahoodaloodaling, blowing their trumpets and banging their drums.

Now and again there were the dark blues and grays of fear, but by the next page, all was gold and rose and glittery stardust.

Children with perfect hair ran past holding pails and shovels. Animals talked to me from the protection of tree limbs, eventually scurrying close and chattering about larger creatures in places not protected by the huge and perfect sun overhead. A farmer, fireman, mermaid came by as I stood by a barn, street, lake.

When the moon rose, it smiled.

There was always a happy ending, even when things were at their most grim. Butterflies, birdsong, baby everything. The hunter found the lost girl; the bird found her nest; the puppy found his mother and siblings; the little girl learned to pick apples. The mermaid promised magic, and she was right.

Those days, I screamed a lot. Night terrors.

"Sometimes, we use punctuation for effect," I told Qiyuan as we sat together at the small round table in the tutoring center. Overhead, a light flickered. Next to us, a student in a cubicle listened to an audio tape about sentence structure, loud enough that we could hear the words "splice" and "fused."

"Sounds like *Frankenstein*." Qiyuan nodded toward the headsetted student and tapped his pencil on the table.

Qiyuan stared at me with no effect or affect, either. He was in a freshman composition class that was about three levels over his skill set, which, when looked at carefully, was impressive: leaving mainland China two years ago, moving to the US, and enrolling in a college. And, apparently, having read *Frankenstein*, though likely in translation.

"Body parts all put together," I said.

"Correct," Qiyuan said, likely in the same tone of his English teacher in Shanghai. He pushed his glasses back against the bridge of his nose, the frames clunky, oversized, stylish. His hair swooshed across his forehead in an elegant swirl, his face smooth, a pepper of mustache on his lip. He smelled like ginger and Red Bull.

"Think of a sentence like the monster. Head. Period. Neck. Period. Sometimes, the middle runs together with chest, heart, stomach. There's not a lot separating them, so we use commas. Legs, knees, and shins are like that, too."

Qiyuan took a sip of his drink, spun his pencil, and pulled the worksheet to him.

"Introductory phrase," he said. "Hello, comma. How are you, question mark."

"Correct," I said.

"I will not understand," Qiyuan said as he skipped right over an opportunity for a perfect Oxford comma. "I will never get A."

I reached out with my pencil, tapping the eggs and fruit and nuts. Comma and comma. He scratched in the mark, and I felt his otherness slide over me like warm oil. He would never understand, at least, not entirely. Whole sections of this life—at college, and in the small town where he rented an apartment with two other international students—would elude him, slipping past. Commas were the least of his worries.

What about me? I was never in one place for long, at least as far as I was concerned. And for everyone else? They thought I'd barely moved, living at home with my mother in her house that grew smaller every year, tutoring at the college I had attended myself, seeing no one really except those I came into contact with at work or in my neighborhood: the postal workers, dog walkers, garbage collectors. My Learning Lab colleagues, English professors, students.

Even that was too much stimulus.

"Good," I said.

I was in the small cottage. In the measly hearth burned a fire, the only warmth and comfort in the room. Next to me, at the table, was my husband, a man worn, a shared daily grind that wound up my back and clenched my neck. So much to do. The animals. The hunting. The work away from home. Stones. Beams. Pounding. And? I raised my reddened hands, strong but sore; wiry but aching. On them, the marks of hard labor, child care, and the tending-to of anything my husband could not.

His eyes were bright blue, an ocean of vision. Here I was married to a man I loved. A good man, a hard worker. At night, the four of us huddled in the bed, grasping for warmth and sleep.

He put a hand on one of mine and then pulled it away as he talked about the new taxes on wheat.

Come back, I thought. Linger.

"Three rabbits," he said, leaning back. "In the traps. But it won't be enough."

"Thought you only brought in two," I said.

My husband shook his head, slumping. "Things gone missing," he said. "A rabbit. A bag of corn, fresh milled, mind you. Things keep getting stolen, we won't have enough for the winter."

I hadn't been hungry all day, tucking aside my need so I could give the last of the bread to my children, but as my husband spoke of all that was absent, my stomach growled.

On the table, the slate I used to teach our children. Blinking, I tried to read the words they'd scratched out before supper, but the letters were fuzzy. Here I needed spectacles we could not afford.

But I liked myself in this story, a woman who had hard work but love and family, too. Of course, there was the thing watching us, but our part in the story was short.

My husband talked on, and I turned toward the back of the room, searching for the crack in the wall. It was always difficult to find. If not, the story would have never progressed, my husband and I poor but not stupid.

"Reverend Jones predicts a colder-than-usual winter. Storms started early," my husband said.

"Terrible," I added, just then finding the crack, a space that opened up to a hovel behind our cottage. My husband used it for storage, but for plot purposes, it was left empty so the monster could come in. And the monster was there now, listening, his grotesque ear pressed to the wooden opening. His large body hulked against wooden slats, waiting, listening, sucking in everything so he could become human.

I stood, as I never did in the real story, and moved into the room, outside of the candlelight.

"We aren't worth it," I said. "Don't think anything you see here is going to help. Leave and never come back."

"What are you saying?" my husband said.

I laughed. "Oh, just talking to the window."

"Crazy woman. Off to bed with us."

"Go." I stared straight at the crack in the wall and turned back toward the light. "Head for the hills. Stay there."

The moment I opened our front door, I scuttled in, feeling the slice and slap of box lids and album covers, the flutter of newspaper, the sharp points of cardboard against my face, body, legs. In the kitchen, thankfully, there was room to move. Here and my room were the only places I could take more than three steps before having to flatten myself to almost invisibility.

"Did you bring dinner?" my mother called.

In my hands, take out from Jumbo Burger down the street, her favorite. As with the guys at Delmonico's Pizza and Flora's Fish Shake and Shack, they knew me by sight. Stevie behind the takeout counter had my cell number, which he'd tried to use for more than just food orders.

I put the food on a tray and took it to my mother in what was left of the living room, avoiding her suspicious eyes. Large, tall and powerful, Mom was pillowy, remnants from her solitary pregnancy twenty-four years ago still on her waist.

In all the photos my father had taken of my mother—he now long gone into some other story—my mother was ripe and full. There she was, huge in every picture: sideways in the grocery store aisle, her maternity dress tight, or collapsed and enormous in a chair minutes before going into labor.

"I felt empty," she said of that time. "Then you left me."

Now she grabbed her meal, the greasy paper crinkling as she freed her burger. I plucked a fry from the pile, wincing as my mother chewed. Sometimes, I imagined her a giant hamster, front teeth grinding away.

She stared at me, unsmiling, gray eyes without shine or sparkle. Her wingback chair jutted into the only free space in the room.

"Aunt Pearl called today," my mother said after her first big swallow. "She has plans."

"About what?" I stared at the spines of a dozen National Geographic magazines.

"The taxes," my mother said. "She thinks we should Airbnb this place and live in one of those, you know, hotels that are like apartments. The kind businessmen get when they travel."

"Or businesswomen," I said.

She waved a hand and then picked up her burger again. "Two bedrooms, bathroom, kitchen. That kind of thing."

For the first time that day but for the millionth time in my life, I looked at her. Today she'd maybe brushed her hair, but her bangs stood up from her wide forehead in a graying corona. She was as pale as milk, her eyes wide. Draped in baggy sweatpants and a loose sweater, her body was wide and big, filling her chair. She smelled like 4,928 days in the same house.

The inside parts of me wanted to wail.

"We could only bring one suitcase each," I said, words carefully placed bricks. "I'd have to call the service again. They would—"

My mother coughed once, twice, the sound a knifing hack. I put down what remained of my fry, stomach churning.

"Not that again." She whispered the words and then picked up her large soda, sucking down the sugar. Her eyes watered, her nose leaked.

Once I'd found a photo of my mother taken when she was in high school. She was on the football field, wearing awkward gym clothes from the eighties. Her dark long hair was pulled back in a ponytail and swung as she ran, her legs long and sexy. In the instant of the shot, she turned back to the person behind the camera and smiled, her teeth white, even, gleaming, her body lithe and slender. Behind her, nothing but sunshine.

She'd thrown open her arms as if wanting to celebrate the air, the grass, the field, the whole world.

Later, when I tried to find the photo, it was gone, disappeared into the flutter of paper, the stacks of LPs, play programs, yearbooks, paperbacks, newspapers, ancient TV Guides, and campaign ads dating from the later eighties. That happy girl was somewhere in this house, trapped along with her hopes, hidden in the looming stacks.

That beautiful girl was my mother's shadow stripe, the kind on a Burchell's Zebra. In between the thick back stripes, there, a light brown line, almost invisible, so light that from a distance, you'd never know it was there.

"So we Airbnb it like this?"

For a moment, both of us surveyed the room, a scene from The Old Curiosity Shop but on obsessive/compulsive steroids. A wacky library with no Dewey Decimal system and an insane librarian.

"I'll tell Pearl she's crazy." My mother dabbed at the corner of her mouth. Her lips were white and cracked, her hands shaking. "Did you get the ketchup?"

It was never the scene from the store in the rain, never the happy reconnection in Bath, England. And certainly, it was never the part when Anne Elliot opens the letter and learns that Wentworth loves her and always has. Not once had she been out at sea with her true love.

No, when I was Anne, I was always in the room with her father Sir Walter Elliot, Lady Russell, Mr. Shepherd, and my sister Elizabeth. Worse, I was always in the third-person, unable to yank Anne into action—the point-of-view unmovable, no wiggle room. No matter how I punched against the pronouns, I was powerless to change things in this story. With more agency, I'd propel her right through the large front entrance, into a carriage, and on her way to points unknown and unwritten.

But here in this room? Unspoken was her father's constant assessment that there was very little to admire about her. Anne wasn't talented, charming, or overly pretty. She hadn't married well or garnered a likely suitor. Worse, she would never appear in any society newspapers, due to her lack of good looks.

She was as important as the brocade chair she sat in, one that would soon be left—along with all their other furniture—when they moved to Bath and let out their ancestral home.

"Quit Kellynch Hall?" Sir Walter stroked his thinning hair and almost tiptoed around the sitting room. "What would they do without us here? I am lord and master."

"Father," Anne said, as she had for well over two hundred years, every time. "We must retrench."

"You will be greatly missed," Lady Russell began, appealing to Sir Walter's outsized ego. "But this is the best solution. You can let to a likely tenant."

"No advertising!" Sir Walter cried.

"Of course not," said Mr. Shepherd, the family lawyer. "Maybe someone from the navy."

Sir Walter Elliot turned, mouth open in surprise. "A naval officer, rich from the wars."

"Indeed," Mr. Shepherd said, urging Sir Walter forward with this plan. "How surprised and lucky such a man would be to find himself in this house. Of this description!"

Sir Walter clasp his thin hands. "I've always liked the navy."

At that, Anne wanted to rip his head off and wrest this scene into another novel, maybe even *Frankenstein* or maybe *Clockwork Orange*, but the Elliots were doomed by the math problem Sir Walter had created with his horrifying spending habits. His debt was a cloak he wore around his skinny shoulders. Most times, Anne nodded and supported Lady Russell's plan, but today, she rose, a hand on the mantel.

She was so thin. Clearly, whatever she had eaten for breakfast—no clues in the story—hadn't been enough. She was always hungry here, wanting all that she didn't have. Her former suitor, Captain Wentworth, soon to be back in her life but so far away at this moment. The very naval man her entire family had scared off eight years before.

"Anne?" Lady Russell asked. "Do you have another notion of how to economize?"

Anne almost burst into laughter, but instead, brought her handkerchief to her mouth. She swallowed and looked out the window. Green stretch of flowing lawn, rolling hills, and then beyond that the ocean, a whole world completely undiscovered. But something from somewhere else pressed on her, holding her down. She wanted to break down the walls of plot and run out into the mist. But she was as doomed as the Elliots, at least in this chapter.

She turned to Sir Walter, her father, a man no one really cared for, not even Austen, his maker.

"The navy has done so much for us. We must allow them their comforts," she said.

"Let us hope this sailor will be the best-looking sailor I have ever met with," Sir Walter said. Mr. Shepherd laughed.

Anne gripped the fireplace, knuckles white, fingers aching.

"He was to me," she whispered.

After Qiyuan's Thursday afternoon session, I packed up and headed out of the tutoring center into the fall afternoon. I'd walked to school that day, despite a thrum of fear with each step. Who knew what I might feel?

"Steph?"

My heart stuttered. No one had called me by my real name in so long, I'd almost forgotten the sound, the stuttering start, the vowel, the labiodental fricative. Blinking into the afternoon glow, eyes slightly squinted, I turned to find Matt, the tutoring coordinator, running toward me.

He was tall and thin, one click away from Ichabod Crane, saved by strong shoulders, big biceps, and good posture. Maybe he was a more macho, all-grown-up Harry Potter. Matt wore glasses, his brown hair long and slightly shaggy, his face clear and smooth, eyes blue. I avoided looking at him when I walked into work, he of the button-down shirt opened at the neck and the almost-tight jeans. Too long a gaze might lead me into a scene I'd probably been barely able to read in the first place.

My first week at the center, I agreed to a coffee in between tutoring sessions. In the warm clatter of the college coffee shop, Matt spoke of travel, his graduate studies, his large Irish family, five siblings, ancestors in Ireland living in ancient whitewashed cottages.

As we walked back to the center, our hands brushed, probably accidentally, but still, his skin was warm. I could feel the light hair on the back of his hand, his watchband, his shirt sleeve. Matt held the door for me, and as I walked past, I flushed, everywhere, every vein, artery, and organ on high alert.

Matt was gangly but popular with students and staff. Sometimes I saw him chatting with Ronda, a new tutor with long dark hair and small feet. Even in winter, she wore sandals to show off her perfect pedicure. In the mornings, he had coffee with Cindy, who worked the desk. She batted her false eyelashes. Students hung around him in circles, staff in lines. He took his calls outside at a table in the sunlight, waving his arms as he spoke and laughing.

Why did he ask me to coffee?

For weeks after sitting across from him, noting his five freckles, his dark eyebrows, his brown eyes flecked with green, I found myself stuck in a Patricia Highsmith novel, the one she wrote under a pseudonym that involved two doomed female lovers. Later, I was subjected to a whirl of days at the start of *Anna Karenina*. The good news is I never strode through the first pages of *Angela's Ashes*—the hard part, at the start, in that wet, cold, impoverished house. But it was only a matter of time.

I'd promised myself no more.

But what did I do now? I looked up.

Matt stopped and put his hands on his slim hips. He smelled like new soap and reams of fresh paper. Gleaming black pens. Unused staples, fresh thumbtacks. "Not coming to happy hour?"

I never went to happy hour, or not since that one time at that beach-themed place on Broadway. Later, for days, I ended up in Key West on a fishing boat with a crazy fisherman and his hostage.

I hated fishing.

"Um."

"Come on," he said. "I'll take you. Drive you home after."

In the beam of his expression, I wrested away from the dark tunnel that was the rest of my day. My mother, her living room, the echoless thud of our entire house.

"Okay," I said, my hands shaking so hard I stuffed them in my sweater pockets.

"Come on then." He actually took my backpack and put it on. "Glad I parked in Lot 5. This thing weighs a ton."

"Qiyuan has a thing for you." Marissa, an adjunct ESL teacher, put another margarita in front of me. She sat down and flipped back her long hair from her forehead in preparation for drinking. Both our glasses sat next to each other in frosty precision. Somehow, I'd sipped through my first, leaving only ice and a half-inch of salt on the rim.

"He does not." I took the straw from my first drink and put it deep into the second, thinking of nothing but the odd, fruity, death smell of tequila.

It tasted amazing.

"Why wouldn't he? Jeez." Marissa dug into the basket of salty chips. "If you were my tutor, if you know what I mean."

She winked and crunched her chip.

"He needs help with his writing."

"He doesn't need four sessions a week! All with you." Marissa slurped. "I told him to work on commas. Next thing I know, he's talking to me after class about Frankenstein. You've got him watching Jane Austen movies. You've got some magic, sister."

I waved her off and sipped deeply, my entire body relaxing into the chair. Across the wooden table, Matt leaned in as he talked to another tutor, Li, about developmental education in the freshman comp class. All the important words turned into butterflies and flew away, carried off in swirls by the bad music piped into the entire bar area. Somewhere outside, a mariachi band pumped horrible sound into the afternoon air.

The room spun. Matt turned, his face a beam of light.

I took turns carrying them all, but mostly, I carried Lieutenant Jimmy Cross, for weeks, day and night with no respite. Yes, I also carried my weapons, the ones with letters and numbers for names. I carried my ammunition and knives and brass knuckles. I slept in the rain if I slept at all, and every morning, I woke in the jungle, knowing that people in the trees wanted to kill me.

In my pack, on my back, I humped all day, carrying my mother in her wingback chair, our house filled with the past no one cared about, and my own grief for not knowing how to move except into places I didn't belong. I carried my small handful of happiness, Matt, my group of colleagues, Qiyuan smiling when he understood how to place a comma just so.

"Correct!" I said.

I carried the weight of every failure I'd never had because I hadn't gone far enough away to make mistakes. I carried my prison, my curse that was no blessing, horrible plots unfolding day after day.

I carried Cross's letters from Martha, the ones that weren't love letters at all but merely signed Love. I read those over and over again, the way that there was never real feeling, only guilt and hope that Jimmy would come back alive. But when that happened, Martha knew all along, she wouldn't be his.

Worse, every day, no matter what, Lavender died, shot in the head on his way back from taking a leak. And it was Cross's fault. My fault. I stopped paying attention, thinking about Martha and how she didn't love me, and the guy was dead. Every time, I thought about Martha, and every time, Lavender was dead.

We all got problems, Norman Bowker said.

A real pisser, Kiowa said.

Maybe it was, but I tried to not feel a thing, to walk through the story, ignoring it all. The death, the weather, my own body, wanting to become as invisible as air, as fake as all this reality was.

When I finally yanked myself back, I reached out and grabbed my phone, reading the date through a hazy eye. Only a night had passed since happy hour, but I was months gone, an ache of time in my whole body. I put the phone down and pushed myself up and out of my bed. My mother banged past with her heavy walk, stopping by my bedroom door.

I closed my eyes, breath light in my throat, waiting. Would she turn the knob? Would she hulk in and demand things? Would I have to give them over, as I always did? The air held tight as I counted. One, two, three. Then she stomped down the hall and into the kitchen. When I scuttled into the bathroom and forced closed the door, I stared at the mirror. Puffy half-moons of darkness cupped my eyes. My skin was pale, my hair straw. All this could be explained by a hangover from my three margaritas and then visit to Matt's apartment afterward, not to mention my mother's seething when I'd returned.

But unseen, invisible now were the blisters on my feet and hands, the wounds, the scrapes, the heartache. It was the damp and heat and everything I carried forever. It was the loss of people I cared about, that loss mine to bear.

I leaned closer to the mirror, staring into the darkness of my pupils. My expression, the tunnel into my brain and out. What next?

Where it stopped, nobody knew, especially not me. But going out? Drinking with friends? Kissing an attractive man who really seemed to like me?

All that had to stop.

What story was my father in this time? The last time they had visited, it had been in Moby Dick, thankfully not on the Pequod, but in the Spouter-Inn. Not in the horrifying room with Queequeg, but near the bar. They were seamen that visit, watching Ishmael make his slow tour of the place.

Once it was in *Alice in Wonderland*, at a tea party. My father had loved this book, reading it to me long before I was ready.

Another time, for a brief glitch, we found ourselves in *The Trojan Women* before being flung out into *Antony and Cleopatra*. There, for a second, was the venomous snake, tongue darting. But pow, we spun into *Moon for the Misbegotten* before being punted into *Hamlet*. After that horrible play within the play, Hamlet manic and insane, we both came to rest on the shores of *Robinson Crusoe*. Not a Friday in sight.

I hadn't looked for him for a long while after that, avoiding my bookcase, filled with all his favorites. But after taking a shower, I went back to my room and locked the door behind me.

I dried my hair, dressed, sat in front of my bookcase, and reached out.

"You can leave," he said.

We sat in the back row of Jenny Fields's funeral. The main character, T.S. Garp, and his best friend Roberta hunker-hid in a front row. Wearing a ridiculous wig, Garp pressed against Roberta's large feminine bulk. His mother had an enormous following, and Garp wasn't welcome to grieve her, at least not here. But it would be a time before they spotted him, so my father and I could whisper in the back row until Garp was tossed out.

Like most of the mourners, my father and I were nurses, or wearing Jenny's *de facto* uniform: white dress, substantial white hosiery, sensible shoes, small neat cap. The room was packed and smelled like rose water and grief.

How to do it? I wanted to ask but didn't. He might say he left, but had he? He was a visitor to all his favorite stories—those in my second shelf--but he was actually somewhere in corporeal form, sitting at a table or on a couch or in a coma, for all I knew.

In the front of a church, an important and very strong woman began to speak about Jenny Fields.

"Maybe I could leave this plot. But leaving a book doesn't count."

"Are you sure?" If you leave a story you don't like for another, doesn't that count as choice? As volition? Aren't you changing course?"

I remembered him sitting in a recliner, a stack of books at the side. Half the time he wasn't really there, zoning in and out of himself, just as I could. But sometimes, I saw him in our real house, reading a book with his eyes instead of his body. Sometimes, he would look over at me and nod.

"We can't really live here," I said. "There are only spaces that accommodate our visits."

My father shrugged. "Same as out there."

"Any second, we are going to be rushed out of here and disappear from the narrative."

"Same as out there."

Everything he said was true, but not. "Dad."

"Shhh!" whispered one of the nurses.

My father put a kind hand on my knee, gently tapping out the seconds as we stared forward, the way we had often sat together. My father had been the parent to read to me at night, starting when I was a baby, giving me my first adventures.

All those years, my father held a book with one hand, patting me with the other during scary parts. Or at the funny bits, Ramona being a true pest; Tigger bouncing, loving all things; Max roaring back at all the monsters.

"Are you happy out there?" I asked him now.

"I'm not saying it's easier," he said. "But—"

Just then, there was a cry. "Garp!"

As the service ended in anger, Garp was hustled out. My father turned to me kindly with his new soft brown eyes. His wavy hair was neatly pinned under his cap, reminding me of Florence Nightingale.

But he hadn't saved anyone but himself.

"There's no *her*," he said. "Here."

"You left me," I said, my mother's own words.

"I needed to show you it was possible."

The nurses bustled out to follow the crowd, everyone chanting.

"Go where she isn't," he said.

The world started to yank us, fading as we moved outside, into the sky that was winding down and out into a whole new chapter.

"Go," my father said, his words, his nurse face, his blue nursing cape fading as the scene swirled into nothing but air.

"Comma here?" Qiyuan gazed at me, a look I recognized from bad TV romances. I kept my pencil firmly on the page, the sentence strung out so incorrectly.

"Remember this: 'Eats, shoots, and leaves,'" I said.

"Panda," Qiyuan said. "Got it."

Qiyuan went through the page, and I sat back. Across the room, Matt waved from behind the long main desk. Behind him, the clock ticked.

"Oxford commas aren't necessary," Qiyan said, though he'd placed them all perfectly.

One comma, I wanted to tell him, could change an entire story.

In my pocket, my phone vibrated, and I glanced up again at Matt, who winked. As Qiyuan moved on to the next worksheet, I peeked at my phone, reading the message.

Your place?

After college, I'd taken over my mother's car, and now, it sat in functional disrepair, unlocked, at the curb, my bags and clothes and boxes inside. As I walked back toward the house, I didn't carry any takeout bags full of hamburgers or pizza or fried fish. No soda or milk shakes or ice cream. Once in the house, I didn't turn toward the kitchen and her, but went one last time to my room, facing the mirror I'd already taken down and put in the car. There I wasn't.

What I left was the bookcase against the wall and in it, the second row of my father's favorites. In the first, mine. Along with all our stories, I was leaving behind the unpaid taxes, the towering mess, and my mother.

"You're leaving," she said when I walked into the living room. "But you've always been gone. Just like your father."

But I wasn't like my father, exactly. I wasn't leaving a child behind. Only my mother, who had abandoned me a long time ago.

"He left and we never heard a word," my mother said, lifting her hand and then letting it fall back on her lap. "Once I realized he was dead—"

"He wasn't dead," I said.

"And then you went as loopy as he did."

"He isn't dead." All I needed was a book to prove it.

"You believe you won't end up like him," my mother said, her eyes shining. She moved forward in her chair, her body hulking over her thighs as she leaned toward me. I tried not to, but I breathed in her smells: empty cardboard boxes, an unused cookie tin, a broken dresser drawer. "You think you'll be different."

My ears rang. My eyes were dry and tearless. A hundred characters churned inside me. Frankenstein's monster; raging, mourning Jenny Fields nurses; the just-exploded Lavender, flying; Anne Elliot hearing for the hundredth time how she was no good. I was wild, a terrible awful no good thing, flouncing over it all.

My hands grasped at what I would never find in this room. Candlestick, poker, machete, gun. I could already hear what would happen, feel the verbs in my movements, the up and down and through.

"You did it," Matt said when I opened the door of my just-rented apartment. In the middle of the floor, the small hump of all my worldly possessions.

I let him in, watching him take in the place, empty now, but later, a couch, table, chairs. After several shopping trips, pots and pans would sit in neat stacks in the ordered cupboards. Cutlery, cups, cake pans. Pie plates, muffin tins, platters. The fridge filled with healthy food I would prepare myself, no take out, not anymore.

There would be two or maybe three of things, but no more. Sheets, towels, blankets. Things dirtied and then washed and folded. Rugs vacuumed, sinks scrubbed.

In the bedroom, a dresser, a nightstand, a bed, and a man, it would seem.

Everything in my life would be visible.

"This is awesome," Matt said, all of his attention shining directly on me.

What story would save me now?

Girl Gone Rogue

Rachel Ronquillo Gray

If it's wrong to love a boy whose only home is a motorcycle
& the open road, then I'm not right & don't want to be. I wear white

dresses anyway. I sing in a soprano anyway. Everything I say
is a question. I'm so tired of being good. His mother warns me

he will leave, like his father left her, & still, I hike up my dress
& climb onto the back of his bike. I know the leather jacket

he gives me was for another girl. I wear it as if he bought it for me,
breathing big to fill the other-girl-shaped hole. Sleeves too long,

it keeps me warm against the ocean breeze. I walk beside him at
night,
wearing this jacket & holding a white daisy. It's the one thing I know

he picked for me. Everyone tells me he won't last. Would it be so bad
if he didn't & in the end, it was just me. Would it be so bad to spread

myself all over the place, let my dresses rip & fly, leave them tangled
in the weeds. Would it be so bad to love the wind & its wispy fingers

in my unbound hair & its grit on my skin. A heavy thing that sings
between my legs & in my palms, my heart, my everywhere-else.

Would it be so bad to trust my body to keep me alive, to lean into
wicked
curves & switchbacks, to crave a silence filled with birds, highways,
me.

Contributor Comments

Jessica Barksdale, "Storytime"
Jessica Barksdale lives and writes in Oakland, California.
More at jessicabarksdaleinclan.com.

This piece came from two different streams of thought, the biggest being a class I was teaching for Southern New Hampshire University's MFA program. In the class, many of the students had picked *Frankenstein* to read, and I thought how the monster was really a part of his creator's story—not his own. This led me to think how parents—like Victor Frankenstein—try to give their children their stories. As parents, we have to finally get to a place where we see that our children's plots have nothing to do with ours. Thus this oddness!

Roy Bentley, "The Girl Who Survived by Pretending to be a Corpse"
Roy Bentley is the author of Walking with Eve in the Loved City, *a finalist for the 2018 Miller Williams Poetry Prize, and* Starlight Taxi *(Lynx House), which won the Blue Lynx Poetry Prize; a new book,* American Loneliness, *is due out in April of 2019 from Lost Horse Press.*

This was inspired by Truong Thi Le, 30 years old at the time of the My Lai Massacre. She survived the shooting of nearly 700 villagers that day by burrowing under corpses and being still. As someone who served stateside in the Air Force during the Vietnam War, I felt that many of us survived that time in our history as a consequence of the sacrifice of others, and this story spoke to the universality of that need not to see your life forfeited anonymously and without remorse on the part of your killers.

Mary Birnbaum, "Like Home"
A closed captioner by trade, Mary also works on nonfiction from her home in Vista, California.

I began writing "Like Home" when my children were toddlers and my marriage was only just revealing itself for what it is: a tangle of cruelty and mercy. The piece was abandoned soon thereafter and then finished in 2018. For scale, my children are now seven and nine. This writing is of special significance because it represents a sort of launch pad for what would become many (so very many) intervening essays about marriage.

Charlie Brown, "I think you're wrong but"

Charles M. Brown is currently an undergraduate student at Salisbury University. He enjoys film photography and large puzzles.

During a talk with my former boss about racism being alive or dead in our time, I realized that he, like others I've met, wasn't aware that he was racially prejudiced. While talking to him, I began to wonder about him and the others and their thinking that they're in the right, with their prejudiced speech and actions, not aware of their prejudice at all. How sad is that? And where does it come from? When you're prejudiced and harmful without even knowing you are. I'm not sure whether to scold or pity them.

Photo credit: Emmanuel Porquin

Bill Capossere, "The Web"

Bill Capossere lives in Rochester, New York, where he writes essays, short stories, and plays in between ultimate Frisbee games and teaching as an adjunct at two local colleges.

"The Web" came directly out of the situation it describes—my attempt to "rescue" a spider that had hitchhiked into our home via some garden vegetables. As is often the case with good intentions, the rescue went somewhat awry, and the event, such as it was, stuck with me as such things are wont to do. I struggled with turning it into an essay, heading futilely down various writing paths before it finally struck me that the web at the piece's center, and those paths, were the metaphor and structure I'd been vainly looking for.

Dionne Custer Edwards, "Court of Common Pleas"

Find this Ohio girl (lifeandwrite.com, @dcusteredwards) living in a house with four guys (three kids and a spouse), trying to find time to write.

The original working title for this piece was "Family Court," which is an informal term used to describe the domestic division of the Court of Common Pleas, a place that divides families into pieces and procedures. This piece is a note on the human experience: on grievances, regrets, love, and longing; on messiness and second chances.

Meredith Doench, "South Carolina, 2012"

Meredith Doench (meredithdoench.com, @MeredithDoench) teaches writing at the University of Dayton and is the author of the Luce Hansen Thriller Series, which features the novels Crossed, Forsaken Trust, *and* Deadeye.

"South Carolina, 2012" began with a writing prompt from NPR's Three-Minute Fiction contest. I assigned it to my students and joined them in the writing challenge. The piece soon turned into a nonfiction flash about my father. I'd recently spent two weeks at my father's home where I came to understand the gravity of his early onset Alzheimer's. I'd been in denial about the severity of my father's diagnosis, and instances like the ones described in the flash brought me face-to-face with a disease I was completely unprepared to deal with. My father passed away in the Spring of 2014.

Margot Douaihy, "Boom"

Margot Douaihy is the author of Scranton Lace *(Clemson University Press) and* Girls Like You *(Clemson University Press).*

Twitter: @MargotDouaihy.

I think of flash fiction as a criosphinx—a sphinx with the head of a ram. It should charge forward with a narrative thrust but hold space in its heart for a riddle. "Boom," my latest flash fiction piece, was inspired by the imaginative work of Italo Calvino. My goal was to craft an unexpected lyrical story like a Calvino fable with a fairy tale atmosphere woven into the universal desire for purpose.

Bruce Ducker, "The Fabulist of Midtown"

Photo credit: *Jack W. London*

The author of eight novels and a book of short fictions, Bruce Ducker has some eighty poems and stories in literary magazines, including The Yale Review, Southern Review, *and* Poetry Magazine. *He lives in Colorado.*

I've always been interested in literary forms. Every reader has loved a frame story—from Chaucer and Mary Shelley to Roald Dahl and John Fowles. It's irresistible: the diffracted points of view, the contrast of characters on different stages, the tension between the frame and the framed stories, and particularly the boost of authority that occurs when one character on the page stops a second:

He holds him with his glittering eye—
The Wedding-Guest stood still,
And listens like a three years' child:
The Mariner hath his will.

Tyler Dunning, "The Practice of Parting Before the Farewell Even Exists"

Tyler Dunning grew up in southwestern Montana, a place where he gained a feral curiosity that has led him around the world, to nearly all of the US national parks, and to the darker recesses of his own creativity. Find his work at tylerdunning.com.

Since moving to Seattle to live with my partner, Jenene, and at her encouragement, I've started bathing with all the luxuries: Epsom salts, bath bombs, bubbles. My essay begins and ends here, in the tub, recounting Jenene's first true exposure to my depressive tendencies, finding me drunk in a pool of water and confessing there is no circumstance in which my story doesn't end with suicide. Surviving this last spiral, especially during a time of high-profile celebrity suicides, I felt it important to reflect on mental illness in our society from an insider's perspective on the pandemic.

Photo credit: DJ Viernes

Steven Duong, "Between Your Body and the Bedroom"

Originally from San Diego, California, Steven Duong is a Vietnamese American poet whose poems are featured or forthcoming in Academy of American Poets, Columbia Poetry Review, Diode Poetry Journal, *and other venues. He loves his friends and family, though he often subtweets them as @boneless_koi.*

I read Terrance Hayes's most recent book while in a long-distance relationship and it inspired me to write a love sonnet that doesn't understand scale, or at least, one that deliberately sets out to misunderstand it. Under these conditions, minutes are as long as centuries, and the human body does not meaningfully differ from a body of water. The sonnet's architecture seems uniquely suited to housing things that refuse to be housed. "Between Your Body and the Boardroom" is my attempt at holding something without a shape, something both present and absent.

Farnaz Fatemi, "Untranslated"

Farnaz Fatemi is a writer and editor in Santa Cruz, CA. She taught Writing at the University of California, Santa Cruz for over twenty years. Her website is farnazfatemi.com.

"Untranslated" came from a question. I was working on my manuscript, *What Kind of Woman*—poems about childhood loneliness; questions of belonging in Iran and California; and the women I've met in both places. A colleague asked me if I had an opening poem that spoke to the book as a whole. "Untranslated" was my effort to answer that question. Most of my writing arises from a deep impulse to translate the world for myself—the multiple cultural languages I inherited as an Iranian-American as well as the sounds and sights of my childhood. Poetry is my way to find meaning, at the same time as it reminds me how futile it sometimes feels to try.

Ta'riq Fisher, "Birds, Bees"

Ta'riq Fisher is an undergraduate student in the Dramatic Writing program at New York University, where he is working toward earning his BFA.

This story primarily came from the fear of my life changing in one moment. No matter what I do or how I do it, if fate (or whatever you want to call it) has something in store for me, I am guaranteed to receive it, and that is almost entirely out of my control. To explore the anxiety gnawing at me, over the course of a year I created a family and gave them lives to live, people to love, things to fear. And then I gave them one moment that changed everything.

Matthew Fitch, "The Tropic"

Matthew Fitch is a writer and attorney living and working in Hartford, Connecticut. His other work is forthcoming in the New Rivers Press American Fiction *anthology series. Find him at fitchmatthew.com*

I like a character who narrates from a remote place, and I like things that are almost other things. The letter thorn (þ) seems like such a thing: part of modern Icelandic, archaic in English, it is real and unreal, is and no more. I thought of a shy adolescent character who adopts it as part of his complex persona, believing it endows his almost-self with shamanic insight. His best friend, meanwhile, is almost popular, almost athletic, almost ready—with my protagonist—to spread his wings and fly straight at the madly spinning wheel of high school fortune.

AnnElise Hatjakes, "Learning to Ration"

AnnElise Hatjakes is a teacher and writer. Her work has been shortlisted for Green Mountain Review's Neil Shepard Prize in Fiction and has appeared in decomP, Drunk Monkeys, and Juked.

"Learning to Ration" was prompted by a situation familiar to many women. I was grading essays at a coffee shop, concentration pulling my brow into a furrow, when a stranger approached me and suggested that I smile. For this *Photo credit: Jennifer Sande* story, I wanted to concretize the unseen, and consequently unacknowledged, forces that mandate regulating emotional responses for the comfort of others; in this case, that regulation takes the form of World War II-era ration books. This story asks who we believe deserves to feel rage, joy, or pity, and what the permissible reactions to those feelings are.

Sara Henning, "Self-Portrait as an Apostle of Longing"

Find her at sarahenningpoet.com and @SaraDHenning on Twitter.

This crown began as an essay braiding a discussion of genre to my mother's death from colorectal adenocarcinoma. By maintaining a too-critical distance, the piece failed. At the time, I was re-reading Patricia Smith's *Blood Dazzler* and drawn to how form (particularly tanka) could assist the discussion of natural disaster (in this case, the ecological and cultural trauma stemming from Hurricane Katrina). In an interview with Jon Riccio, she said, "You can't look directly at death unless you can contain it. It's horrific in its undefined edges, and the idea of it unleashes a fear that blurs both its reality and inevitability. The tight control of the tanka is . . . a taming of what refuses to be tamed. Working in . . . form didn't change the truth, it just . . . helped me rein in rampaging emotion." Smith made me realized that a vessel was crucial to shaping my thoughts, which lead me back to my love affair with the sonnet.

Photo credit: Hardy Meredith

Faylita Hicks, "Black Escapism"

Faylita Hicks is a black queer writer. She was a 2018 PEN American Writing for Justice Fellowship finalist, a finalist in the 2018 Cosmonaut Avenue Annual Poetry Prize and a finalist for the 2018 Yes Yes Books Open Reading Period. Her debut book, HOODWITCH, is forthcoming October 2019 with Acre Books.

She is on Twitter and Instagram @faylitahicks.

I was sharing memes with some friends when I came across one that pointed out that Black people laugh differently, sometimes with our whole bodies. It made me think about Black joy and how throughout our history, our joy has been labeled dangerous or frightening by those who do not understand our extreme and nuanced reactions to humor or good news. In this poem, I try to describe how joy is what allows us to deal with the many kinds of pains that come with living in the Black body; how—in a way—it prepares us for death.

Daniel Lassell, "Finishing the Harvest"
Daniel Lassell appears recently in Post Road, Lunch Ticket, Frontier Poetry, Permafrost, *and* Yemassee.
Visit his website at daniel-lassell.com.

Photo credit:
Austin Lassell

"Finishing the Harvest" stems from my experience growing up on a llama and alpaca farm in Kentucky. To reduce the cost of purchasing feed and hay during the winter, my family would assist one of our neighbors during harvest season and receive a portion of his hay bales. When my parents divorced, we lost the farm. In recent poems, I've been exploring how presence does and doesn't factor into the healing process, and what it means to cultivate and lose things. This poem is a part of that exploration.

Katherine Lo, "God's Ears"
Katherine Lo is a writer and high school English teacher in Southern California.

What started out as a playful reworking of the famous thought experiment somehow became a meditation on the human longing to be heard and known. I was raised with the belief (and still cherish the hope) that there is a God who hears us and listens, but I wrestle with how disjunct that immaterial reality is from my own primarily physical existence. So I put God's ears in the most concrete images I could think of at the time.

Daniel Lusk, "Self-Portrait with Cat"
Daniel Lusk is author of six poetry collections, the most recent The Vermeer Suite *and* The Shower Scene from Hamlet.
He lives in Vermont with his wife, Irish poet Angela Patten.

First, the cat. This thread echoes the nursery rhyme that ends: "How many were going to St. Ives?" Also something I learned from lines of Thomas Merton's poem "Evening: Zero Weather"—There is no bird song there, no hare's track / No badger working in the russet grass. Each object registers in our minds before being erased, so a ghost image (palimpsest) or sense remains. So the cats remain, reaffirmed by the memory of neighbor Boone, but maybe (as with the girl / muse and pebbles, who may not have been at all) as a wistful, imaginary aspect.

José Enrique Medina, "A Restaurant in Guadalajara"
Find Medina on Facebook at facebook.com/henry.medina.1865.
On vacation in Guadalajara with my brother, I found a restaurant. The food was so delicious that it struck up memories of home, memories of being children and being loved by mother. It was so strange to feel unmoored and comforted at the same time. Food can bring back childhood memories, emotions that we had long forgotten. I wanted to write a short, concise piece that captured that experience. At the same time, I wanted to celebrate the roots of my Mexican culture.

Rachel Ronquillo Gray, "Good Girl Gone Rogue"
A Kundiman, VONA, and Pink Door fellow, Rachel Ronquillo Gray lives in Indiana where she writes and makes a lot of food. You can find her at medusaironbox.com and on Instagram or Twitter @medusaironbox.
This poem grew out of one of my favorite lines from the John Waters film *Cry-Baby*, as spoken by Allison, the good girl character: "I'm so tired of being good." In my work and in this particular poem, I'm interested in peeling back the layers of the "good girl" trope and exploring the desires and voices that lie underneath that facade. So much of the "good girl" trope is based on paternalistic ideas of purity, obedience, and propriety; with this poem, I wanted the Good Girl to give them all the finger and say, "Watch what I can do."

Eleanor Stern, "The Bargain"
Visit Eleanor at eleanorstern.com, and follow her on Instagram @eleanorstern3.
I wrote "The Bargain" slowly, over the course of a long, sweltering summer by myself in London. I knew nobody in town, and it was the first time I'd been alone for any extended period since the loss of a close friend about six months before. I found myself thinking about the strange ways that loss, and the memory of loved ones, can twist in the brain, especially when one is surrounded by strangers and cut off from the people who share those memories.

Photo credit:
Jonah Goldman Key

Hannah van Didden, "Jezabel's Reformation"

Hannah does not know the end of a story when she begins to write it. You will find more of her at 37thirtyseven.com.

I have spent much time interrogating the (his)tories and myths I was led to believe as a child; Jezabel's story was not consciously in my scope. In writing this fiction, Jezabel appeared on the page, demanding to be spelt with an a, inspiring me to seek out her story—which I discovered was, as for many Biblical characters, the result of a thin filtration through particular ideals. Considering her story brings me to wonder: what is real and true and important, and how does this bear on our beliefs?

Photo credit: Suzy-Lou

Jenna-Marie Warnecke, "Cuddlebug"

Jenna-Marie Warnecke's fiction, poetry, and essays have been featured in publications including F(r)iction, Washington Square Review, *and* Narratively. *She lives in New York City.*

A friend referred to my partner at the time as "Cuddlebug," and I imagined a company of professional cuddlers, going around town comforting people in a physical but nonsexual way. I wondered, what would inspire a person to do this? What kinds of people would hire them? It took me awhile to find the right voice for Michael; he started out cynical, bitter, faking his cuddles, but the story was a slog to write and absolutely no fun. Then I thought: maybe I should go the opposite direction, and allow him to be incredibly, deeply sincere. Then the fun began.

Photo credit: Loraine Walters

Photo credit: Loraine Walters

About the Cover

"Self-Portrait," Sonia Brittain

As a child, I loved drawing and painting; it is what I naturally gravitated to, despite the fact that no one in my immediate family was particularly into art or supportive of a career in the arts. I ended up studying medicine at university and specialized in psychiatry. During those years as a doctor working in London, I did not draw or paint at all, and I really started to miss sketching. It was not until after I had my third son and we moved to Switzerland that I finally became more consistent in drawing again. Committing to a drawing-a-day project in 2014 provided the motivation for me to allow myself to make time for art every day. It also resulted in me finding an online art community via Instagram that shared a love of making time for creativity too. I feel, looking back over time, I have changed so much and become so much more confident in drawing and painting. My sketchbooks show my development and changing interests, though some muses still remain—I still love to draw my children, and sketching people has always been a fascination. I sometimes wonder if I am drawn to figurative art in a similar way that I was drawn to studying psychiatry—I have always been interested in human relationships and listening to other people's stories. The best portraits for me are the ones that make you want to know about the sitter or even inspire you to imagine your own story—which is what happens to me when I am drawing someone I don't know. The piece on this cover is a self-portrait, a gouache study of me turning my head away on top of an old heavily patterned painting that I didn't like and was about to throw away. At the time I don't think I was thinking particularly deeply about it, but looking at it now it makes me think about how we all have aspects of ourselves that we don't like or want to change. I have succeeded in changing the original painting, which at one point I just wanted to rip up. Changing ourselves is sometimes more diffi-cult—and we can often remain a mystery to ourselves. I am drawn to paint-ings of subjects turning away because—as both a viewer and as a painter—they allow me to put more of my interpretation and mood onto the painting.

Maybe it's due to life experience, maybe the fact that I have got into a habit, but now making art is essential. I still primarily make art for myself. I find it therapeutic, like a form of meditation. For me, I feel most myself and content being in the moment, making marks with a pen, pencil or with paint. My sketchbooks contain so many memories; often, looking back through them, I can see clearly where I was and what I was doing at the time. Sometimes they evoke a clearer sense of place, of smell, or feelings than a photo might. I think that is one of the special things about drawing—often it makes you observe things more closely and appreciate small details that you might otherwise ignore. The images of my sleeping children are especially precious to me. Lately, as the children are getting older and I am becoming more confident, I have started to focus more on certain areas. I have begun painting landscapes on a larger scale. I am currently influenced by views of the bay area, near where I live. I want these paintings to evoke a sense of atmosphere. I also still love figurative art and have continued to draw and paint portraits. With these, I want to improve in attaining a likeness. Yet at the same time, I want them to remain painterly or a sketch—to make the viewer wonder about the person depicted, or want to look more at the lines or brushstrokes used. My latest project has been to start painting abstracts, and I have a daily abstract journal where I allow myself to explore mark making and color.

When I worked in psychiatry, I knew a consultant psychother-apist who had a Rothko in her room. It makes sense that this type of art is so appealing in various settings, because it allows the artist to put their emotions into a piece, to express themselves with color, marks—yet it may still remain a mystery to the viewer and each person view-ing it may see or feel different things than someone else. That is the joy of art for me: there is always so much to explore, so many ways to depict emotions, places, relationships, life. The possibilities are endless.

41423978R00086

Made in the USA
Middletown, DE
07 April 2019